Lawson carefully
floor. "Blood."

Ashlee stood by the door, reluctant to enter. Her face paled and Lawson thought she must be remembering something. Was being here sparking some memory? Somewhere deep in her subconscious, she knew what had gone down here. She only needed to recall it.

He walked over to her. "You okay?"

She looked around, anguish on her face as she shook her head. "Nothing is coming back. Something happened here, though, didn't it?"

"More than likely. No one reported hearing any gunfire from here, but this place is so far out and so isolated it's unlikely anyone would have heard it. If they did, they probably didn't think anything about it. It's not unusual to hear gunfire in this area."

"What does that mean for my sister?" Ashlee locked eyes with him. "How is this good for her?"

It wasn't, but Lawson didn't want to say that...

Virginia Vaughan is a born-and-raised Mississippi girl. She is blessed to come from a large Southern family, and her fondest memories include listening to stories recounted around the dinner table. She was a lover of books from a young age, devouring tales of romance, danger and love. She soon started writing them herself. You can connect with Virginia through her website, virginiavaughanonline.com, or through the publisher.

Books by Virginia Vaughan

Love Inspired Suspense

Cowboy Lawmen

Texas Twin Abduction

Covert Operatives

Cold Case Cover-Up
Deadly Christmas Duty
Risky Return
Killer Insight

Rangers Under Fire

Yuletide Abduction
Reunion Mission
Ranch Refuge
Mistletoe Reunion Threat
Mission Undercover
Mission: Memory Recall

No Safe Haven

TEXAS TWIN ABDUCTION

VIRGINIA VAUGHAN

LOVE INSPIRED SUSPENSE
INSPIRATIONAL ROMANCE

LOVE INSPIRED® SUSPENSE
INSPIRATIONAL ROMANCE

ISBN-13: 978-1-335-72176-1

Texas Twin Abduction

Copyright © 2020 by Virginia Vaughan

Recycling programs
for this product may
not exist in your area.

This is a work of fiction. Names, characters, places and incidents are either the
product of the author's imagination or are used fictitiously. Any resemblance
to actual persons, living or dead, businesses, companies, events or locales is
entirely coincidental.

This edition published by arrangement with Harlequin Books S.A.

For questions and comments about the quality of this book, please contact us
at CustomerService@Harlequin.com.

Love Inspired
22 Adelaide St. West, 40th Floor
Toronto, Ontario M5H 4E3, Canada
www.Harlequin.com

Printed in U.S.A.

There is therefore now no condemnation to them which are in Christ Jesus, who walk not after the flesh, but after the Spirit.
—Romans 8:1

This book is dedicated to my friend and writing buddy, Diane Ashley, whose encouragement and support over the years have kept me reaching for my goals. Thank you, my friend.

ONE

Deputy Lawson Avery was counting down the minutes until the end of his shift when he could go back to his ranch. He'd given this law-enforcement gig a try, but it wasn't for him. He'd much rather be in jeans and boots than a uniform and could only be grateful that this was his last assignment.

He'd agreed to take this one last shift to appease his brother, Josh, the current sheriff of Courtland County, Texas, when Josh had called him in to sub for a deputy out with the flu.

Lawson had given being a deputy the same chance he'd given the other four jobs he'd taken in the past few years to try to find his place. He'd gone through the police academy, gotten his certifications and given the job eight months before deciding it wasn't for him. He was more and more convinced that his place was at Silver Star Ranch. He'd never wanted anything other than managing his family's twenty-six acres. His ex-fiancée had called him unambitious for not wanting something more, and he'd spent the past few years trying to prove her wrong until he'd finally realized that she was right. Ranching was in his blood and Silver Star Ranch had been in the family for six generations of Averys. His deepest desire was to keep that legacy going. If that was unambitious, then so be it.

His radio squawked, relaying a call about an abandoned car on the side of Boyce Canyon Road. He was only two miles away so he responded to Dispatch that he would check it out. He'd make sure it was his last official act as a deputy sheriff before he hung up his star for good.

He rounded a corner and spotted the abandoned vehicle. It was half on the shoulder and sticking out into the lane. A definite hazard to oncoming traffic. He switched on his lights to alert anyone rounding the curve and was about to run the license plate when he noticed something unusual. The back of the car was riddled with what looked like bullet holes. Someone had been shooting at this car.

He used his radio to call in the make, model and license plate, and also mentioned the bullet holes. He didn't recognize the car and his instincts were on high alert. They only spiked higher when, as he approached, weapon at the ready, he spotted someone slumped over on the front seat. Long dark hair covered the face, but he could see from the petite form it was a woman. He checked the backseat and saw nothing. No one else was inside, but a purse and a duffel bag sat on the front floorboard.

"Ma'am?" Lawson knocked on the window and called to the woman. She was eerily still and didn't respond to him. "Ma'am? Can you hear me?"

He tried the door and found it unlocked. He touched her arm and she let out a soft moan. She was alive. "Ma'am, can you hear me?"

She moved and he jerked backward. Suddenly, she sat up and glanced around. When she pushed the hair from her face, he gasped.

Ashlee!

He holstered his gun and knelt beside her. "Ashlee, it's Lawson. Can you hear me?"

She turned to look at him, dazed and visibly confused. There was a gash on her forehead near her hairline. "What happened?"

"You tell me. Are you okay?"

She shook her head, but he thought it was more to clear it than to respond to his question. She grimaced and touched her fingers to her forehead. "Are you hurt?" he added.

She checked herself. "My head hurts, but otherwise I—I don't think so." She looked at him. Her eyes were just as deep a green as ever, albeit clouded with puzzlement at the moment. "What…what did you call me?"

"I called you Ashlee." Was she having trouble hearing him? He'd heard that some head injuries could cause a ringing in the ears.

"Do I know you?"

That stung. "Considering we used to be engaged, yeah, you know me. Lawson Avery?"

"Engaged?" He still couldn't be sure she was hearing everything he was saying… but there was no mistaking the confusion in her expression. Or the lack of recognition. "Where am I?"

It didn't make sense that she didn't know him. They'd been a couple for years and very nearly married before she'd left him the day before their wedding to pursue her career in the big city.

True, it had been six years since then—but surely that wasn't long enough for her to forget him completely. Then he remembered her sister, Bree. Her identical twin sister. She'd left town over ten years ago and hadn't even returned for the wedding-that-wasn't. Even though they'd all grown up together, he supposed he might have changed enough in ten years to be harder to place. Was it possible he was talking to her instead? "Bree? Is that you?"

She glanced at him again, still confused. "I thought you said my name was Ashlee."

Understanding dawned and he pressed her. "Don't you know your own name?"

Anger flashed in her eyes. "Of course I do." Yet he saw her mind turning over and over, looking for answers, until tears pooled in her eyes. "I don't. I don't know who I am."

Amnesia. Possibly from whatever had caused those bullet holes—or maybe from hitting her head.

He used his shoulder mic to call Dispatch for an ambulance before questioning her further.

"Do you remember what happened? How did you get here?"

Panic set in and her breathing grew heavy. "I don't know. I can't remember."

He reached in for her hand, noticing it was still small and delicate in his. "It's okay. We'll figure it out. We'll figure it out." He gestured to the purse on the floorboard. "Maybe your identification is in there."

She snatched it up and dumped the contents onto the seat, grabbing for the wallet. She opened it, then handed it to him.

He focused on the driver's license. Ashlee Taylor. Just as he'd thought. But how had she ended up in a shot-up car stranded on the side of the road here in Courtland County? Her parents no longer lived here, and she wasn't close to anyone in town anymore. There was little reason for her to come back home for the first time in six years.

Little reason except him.

Stop it. Their relationship had ended the day she'd fled town, leaving him only a hand-written note and a broken heart. She'd said she couldn't live her life in a backwater town. She wanted a big-city life and someone with ambition to be more than a rancher.

She'd ripped out his heart and hadn't looked back.

Now she was in town again and needed his help.

The ambulance arrived and took Ashlee to the hospital for evaluation. She clung to her wallet despite the paramedics' attempts to take it from her. She needed it. She needed it to remind her who she was. They finally relented and let her keep it with her as they arrived at the hospital and she underwent an examination.

How could she not know her own name? And why did it sound so foreign to her ears even when she stared at it on her driver's license—or when that deputy had said it?

"Lawson" was more familiar to her than her own name. Something about the kindness in those blue eyes settled her. He seemed familiar, but she didn't know why. *Maybe because you used to be engaged to him.* Then why couldn't she remember him?

He knocked on the door of her hospital room and peeked his head inside as the doctor finished up his exam. "Do you feel like talking?" Lawson asked.

She was glad to see him, glad to have someone around that she—sort of—recognized. But when he entered, a woman walked in behind him.

"Ashlee, this is Cecile Bradley. She's an investigator with the sheriff's office. She'd like to ask you some questions."

Ashlee folded her arms over her chest. She didn't want to answer any questions, mostly because she was positive she didn't have any answers. She didn't know what had happened to her.

But Cecile's tone was kind and understanding. "Tell me the last thing you remember."

She tried to recall, but the only memory she had was of waking up in her car and hearing Lawson's voice calling to her. She'd been comforted by his presence despite the fear of not being able to remember what had happened to her or even her own name.

But something was terribly wrong. A sense of dread crawled up her neck and tears pooled in her eyes. She didn't know what had occurred or how she'd ended up in that car, but she knew something awful had happened.

"We're inspecting your car, Ashlee, and there are bullet holes in the back, like someone was shooting at you as you drove away. Do you remember anything about that?"

She tried to push past the block of nothingness, but she couldn't. "I don't know. I don't remember."

"Well, we're still examining it. Maybe we'll find something that helps." Cecile glanced at the doctor by the bed. "How is she, Doc?"

The doctor looked to Ashlee and raised his eyebrows, silently asking for her agreement to share her medical results. She nodded. "Physically, she's fine. A small gash on her head, a light concussion, but no other injuries. If she was in the car when those shots were fired, then whoever was shooting at her didn't hit her."

"Why can't she remember anything?" Lawson asked.

The doctor looked to Ashlee again, and this time, she decided to answer directly. She may not know much about herself, but she was already pretty sure she didn't like having others discuss her situation as if she wasn't even there.

"They've told me it's probably psychological—a result of emotional trauma from whatever happened to me," she said. "My mind has blocked it out in order to protect itself."

"What are the chances of her remembering?" Lawson asked the doctor.

Ashlee felt a little frustrated that he seemed so determined to have this conversation *about* her, but not *with* her. Was there a reason he didn't want to engage with her directly?

Engage. Suddenly, she remembered his words from earlier. *Considering we used to be engaged, yeah, you know me.* Okay, so maybe he did have reasons to avoid talking to her.

"I really can't say. That'll take some time." The doctor nodded goodbye to them all. "I'll check in on you later, Miss Taylor," he said, then walked out.

Cecile turned back to her. "Ashlee, we want to check into your background and your financials to try to see if we can figure out what you've been doing and why someone might want to hurt you. Is that okay with you?"

She gave her permission. She, too, wanted to know, and hoped they'd uncover something that would help her piece together whatever was going on.

Lawson and Cecile left and Ashlee leaned back into the pillow and tried to think. This was all so confusing. She didn't understand what was happening—but she knew she didn't like it. Bullet holes? Amnesia? What was going on with her?

She felt the sedative the nurse had just given her start to take effect and sank deeper into the covers. The nurse had turned down the lights and left Ashlee alone to rest, but her mind was racing too fast to relax. All she could think of was Lawson and the soft lift of his voice as he'd called her name when she'd first awoken.

How could she have been engaged and not remember it? Not even remember the man she'd once loved. Still loved? No, he'd said they *used* to be engaged—making it clear that they weren't anymore. Something must have happened to break them up. Maybe she didn't even want to see him. That made her feel even more alone. She didn't like it.

The door opened, but she didn't react to it. In the few hours since she'd arrived, nurses and medical assistants had been in and out on a regular basis. That's what happened in hospitals. Great. She could remember what a hospital was like, but not even if she'd ever been in one before. It wasn't fair.

The light flowed in through the door, breaking into the darkness that soothed her. She hoped the nurse or whoever was there left soon. She felt someone reach over her head to her pillow. It didn't need fluffing and she almost angrily said so, her nerves were so on edge. She opened her eyes and cold, hard ones looked back. She didn't recognize the man who stood over her, but instantly registered him as a threat.

He grabbed the pillow from behind her and shoved it over her face before she could react. Fear ripped through her as she realized she was being attacked. He was trying to kill her!

She pushed at his arm, but her efforts didn't move him. Panic mixed with fear as she knew her time was limited. She struggled and flailed, but nothing helped. He easily outweighed her.

Her life didn't flash before her eyes. Nothing flashed before her eyes. Everything was still blank and she didn't understand why this was happening to her.

God, please help me!

She was going to die, after all.

Lawson headed toward Ashlee's hospital room. He shouldn't have come back here. He shouldn't even care what happened to her... but he couldn't just dismiss her after what she'd been through, could he? He'd loved her once. He'd almost married this woman. He couldn't leave her to face alone whatever she'd gotten into. There had to be a reason she was in his town. A part of him hoped she'd been coming to see him—that she'd known that despite their broken engagement, he'd still do whatever he could to help her combat the danger she now faced.

The hairs on the back of his neck shivered a caution before he even reached her room and his anxiety kicked up a notch. He pushed open the door. A man standing at Ashlee's bedside was holding a pillow over her face. He was suffocating her.

"Stop!" Lawson shouted, reaching for his weapon as he approached, only to realize it wasn't there. He'd left it in his locker back at the sheriff's office once his shift had ended.

The man spun around and Lawson grabbed him, pulling him off Ashlee. The attacker stumbled backward, the pillow still in his hand, and Ashlee sat up, gasping for breath. The man tossed the pillow, then shoved Lawson against the wall, slamming his head against the window blinds. Lawson heard glass break. Momentarily dazed by the impact, he wasn't able to react quickly enough as the assailant bolted for the door.

Lawson scrambled to the bed to check on Ashlee. Another few moments and that man would have killed her.

"Are you okay?" he asked her.

She couldn't speak, but nodded in response to his question.

He hit the nurses' emergency call button, then turned and ran from the room, chasing after the guy. He hadn't gotten a good look at him, but the man had been wearing a white doctor's coat. Lawson hurried down the hall, but didn't see him. He checked in the stairwell, only to find the lab coat tossed on the floor. The guy was gone and he'd shed the only item Lawson could list in a description.

He rushed back to Ashlee's room where a team of nurses was already helping her.

"Sir, I'm going to have to ask you to stay

outside," one of the nurses said, trying to push him from the room.

But Lawson refused to be budged. "I walked in and found a man smothering her with the pillow. I chased after the guy, but he got away. Is she okay?"

The nurse nodded. "Looks like you found her in time."

He couldn't believe it. An attack on her right here in the hospital. He shook his head as the full realization of what was happening sank in. Ashlee was in serious trouble. Someone wanted her dead.

At a nurse's insistence, and only after she'd promised someone would stay with Ashlee at all times, he went downstairs to the emergency room for an examination, since his head had slammed into the glass window. He texted Josh about the attack, and his brother was at the hospital in a flash, yanking open the curtain to the exam room and demanding to know what was happening.

"I'm fine," Lawson insisted once he told his brother about confronting the attacker.

The doctor who'd examined him concurred. "I don't see any evidence of a concussion and nothing that needs stitches. You're free to go, Deputy."

Lawson thanked him, then stood up. His

head was aching from the bump, but he was more concerned about Ashlee and discovering who was after her than he was about the pain.

"Can you give a description?" Josh asked him.

Lawson felt his neck redden as he shook his head. "Not really, no. It happened so fast and the room was dark. He was a big guy."

"What about the victim? Could she identify him?"

"I haven't had the opportunity to ask. The nurses and doctor are still with her."

"Okay, let's head down to the security office and have them pull the video. Maybe they captured an image of him. Then we'll go back upstairs to get her statement."

He went with his brother and waited while the security guard located and pulled up the footage.

"There he is," Lawson stated confidently when he spotted a figure in dark clothes heading toward the exit after the attack. The man kept his face hidden as he walked and had his hat pulled low over his face. He pushed through the front entrance doors and disappeared into the parking lot.

The security guard pulled up another

image of the parking lot and they watched the guy get into a car and drive off.

"Can we get another image of that car?" Josh asked.

The security officer shook his head. "Our equipment isn't that sophisticated. That's the best image we have. That's visitor parking, too, so it's not assigned to anyone in particular."

"We can't get a license plate, but I'll issue a BOLO for the make and model," Josh stated, referring to the be-on-the-lookout bulletin.

"Can you pull up the video of the hallway from before the attack? Maybe we can catch an image of him entering the room."

The security guard nodded and pulled up the requested video.

Lawson spotted the man, wearing the same dark clothes, but without the hat and, this time, wearing the white doctor's jacket. "That's him."

The figure on the screen kept his head down and his face hidden as he approached the door to Ashlee's room. They wouldn't capture an image of his face from this angle, either, but Lawson did notice the man didn't hesitate as he entered Ashlee's room to kill her.

Josh turned to Lawson. "This image isn't

much, but we'll send it out, anyway. Maybe someone will recognize him. Let's go talk to the victim."

They got on the elevator and Lawson knew he had to tell his brother the full story of what was happening before they reached Ashlee's room.

"There's something you should know about her, Josh."

"This is the same lady you found on the side of the road, right?" It was obvious he had no idea who he was about to encounter.

"Yes, it is."

"Well, this just confirms that someone is after her. Has she said anything else about what's happening to her?"

"Not as far as I know—last I heard, she still doesn't remember anything."

"Well, this attack may have shaken something loose. Maybe she recognized the guy."

The elevator doors opened and they both stepped out. Josh headed down the hall, but Lawson didn't follow him. His brother turned back to him. "Are you coming?"

"Josh, the woman who was attacked… The victim…"

"What about her?"

"It's Ashlee Taylor."

He saw his brother's demeanor change as

recognition sunk in. Josh gave a long sigh, then stepped back toward Lawson and leaned against the wall. "Ashlee. Are you sure?"

Of course, he was sure. "I think I'd know her when I see her."

"Sure, but… She has a twin, doesn't she? And from what you've told me, it's not like she remembers her name."

"She was carrying Ashlee's identification and driving a car registered to Ashlee Taylor. It's Ashlee. I'm sure of it."

Josh gripped his shoulder. "How are you holding up?"

"I'm okay. I'm dealing with it. I just wanted you to know before you walked into that room."

Josh slapped him on the back, then morphed into cop mode and headed down the hall. By the time Lawson caught up to him, he'd walked inside and greeted Ashlee.

She still looked pale, but her color seemed to be returning with the assistance of an oxygen mask.

"You probably don't remember me," Josh said, pulling up a stool, "but I'm Lawson's brother, Josh. I'm also the sheriff now."

She stared at him a moment, then slowly shook her head. "I'm sorry. I don't recognize you."

A part of Lawson was relieved. If she had known his brother and not him, that would have awoken jealousy inside him. It made no sense, but he was glad regardless. Yes, it was petty, but he couldn't help it.

"That's okay," Josh told her. "Let's talk about the man who attacked you here. Did you know him?"

She shook her head. "I didn't really get a good look at him, but he didn't seem familiar."

Josh pulled out the photo he'd gotten from the video surveillance and showed it to her. "Take a look at this. Are you sure you haven't seen him before?"

She shrank back at the image, but shook her head. "I don't know who that is."

"But you believe he's dangerous, don't you? You flinched when you saw him."

"Well, he did just try to kill me."

"Tell me what happened."

"I was trying to sleep. He came in and grabbed the pillow and put it over my head. I thought I was going to die until Lawson grabbed him and fought him off. Once the pillow was gone, I was too busy trying to get my breath back to notice much of anything. I heard a struggle, but I didn't look up. I didn't even see him run off."

"And you're certain you haven't seen him before?"

"I haven't—not as far as I can remember, anyway." She glared at him. "You think I'm faking? I'm not. I honestly don't know why this is happening."

Josh stood. "Okay. Well, I'm sure you'll be released soon. Do you have somewhere to stay? Where can we contact you if we have more questions?"

Fear rustled through her eyes as she seemed to realize that she had no plans.

"Don't your parents still own property in town?" Josh suggested.

"That house isn't livable," Lawson said. "It's been abandoned for nearly ten years." Nature, he knew, had taken it back after her parents and sister had moved away. Though Ashlee had remained in town, she hadn't liked staying in the house alone and had found an apartment closer to town. The plan had been for her to live there until they'd married and she moved to the ranch. That, of course, had never happened.

"It's fine," she told them both. "I'll just go to a hotel."

A hotel was a sensible solution. His instinct had been to take her to the ranch, but that wasn't a good idea. Josh and his other brothers would surely have had something to say about that.

And they were all home now, having taken time off while their father recovered from a heart attack. Lawson's sister had already left to return to her job. Miles would leave next to return to the Marshals Service and Colby would be heading out in a few days to return to his job with the FBI. But no matter where they were located, they would have opinions on his letting Ashlee back into his life—and they would be right. Ashlee may be a blast from the past, but she was a painful one and he wasn't so sure he was ready to deal with that 24/7.

Josh stood. "It's good to see you again, Ashlee. Don't worry. We'll figure out what's going on here."

She thanked him and he walked out.

Lawson followed him out and Josh stopped to ask him a question once they were outside the closed door. "Do you believe her about the amnesia?"

"I do." He'd seen no hint of recognition in her face about anything. She'd blocked it all out. "The doctor concluded it wasn't a head injury. He thinks it's caused by an emotional traumatic event. She saw or experienced something that was so terrible she had to block it out to survive."

Josh put away his notebook. "We'll figure it out. I'm going to start digging into her financials and GPS on her car. Maybe we can sort out where she's been."

He nodded. "I'm sure Cecile is already on top of that."

"Okay, I'll check with her."

The elevator dinged as they were heading toward it and Cecile stepped off.

"We were just talking about you," Josh stated. Cecile had been with the sheriff's office for three years and had worked her way up to the position of his brother's chief deputy.

Lawson noticed she was holding the duffel bag from Ashlee's car. "Is that Ashlee's bag?"

"It sure is. I thought you both should see it." She knelt down, unzipped the bag and opened it. Inside was a boatload of cash—all in small bills.

Lawson was stunned by the sight, his mind rushing through all the reasons Ashlee might be carrying that much cash around. None of them was good. He knelt, glanced at the bag and then back at Ashlee's room.

What had she gotten herself into?

Josh plopped the unzipped bag onto her hospital bed. Ashlee was surprised to find the bag full of cash.

"Wh-what is this?" She had no idea why they were showing her this.

"This bag was in your car," Lawson told her. "Any idea why you were carrying all this money with you?"

She reached out and touched it, but shook her head. It didn't look familiar, either. "I don't know." She couldn't even imagine why she would need so much cash—or where she would have gotten it. She glanced at their faces. This made them even more suspicious about what she was involved in. Why couldn't she remember? Why didn't she know what this was for?

"I don't know," she said, pushing the bag away, an irritated edge in her voice at their pressing stares.

Cecile zipped the bag. "We counted it. It's twenty-five thousand dollars in small bills."

They were staring at her, waiting for her to explain, but she had no explanation. She didn't know what the money was for or where it had come from. "I told you. I don't know."

She pulled the blankets up near her neck, recalling the feeling of not being able to get air. She'd nearly died, and this money was probably connected to the reason why she was in danger—maybe someone was after her for the money, or maybe she'd gathered a lot of cash to run from whoever was chasing her—but she had no idea what the truth was. "I'm tired now. I'd like to rest."

Cecile glanced at Josh who was still staring Ashlee down. There was no understanding on his face—just suspicion. He had a grudge against her for sure. It had to be because of the broken engagement with his brother, not that she remembered anything about that, either. She had no explanations and it frustrated her as much as it did them.

Finally, Josh nodded and Cecile lifted the bag off the bed. "I'll keep looking." She and Josh walked out of the room, but Lawson remained behind.

Tears pushed at her eyes, threatening to let loose, but she held them back. Regardless of what he'd said, he was a stranger to her and she wasn't comfortable enough to cry in front of him. "They don't believe me."

"They're used to pushing people to get answers. Sometimes it helps."

"Well, it doesn't help me to be pushed." A tear slipped through and down her cheek and she angrily wiped it away. She didn't want to be in this position. "I don't know anything. I can't remember what happened to me. I don't know who was shooting at me or why or what that money was for. I don't remember."

He reached for her and pulled her to him as the tears began to break through. "It's okay, Ashlee. I believe you."

She sucked in the musky scent of his aftershave and it sent familiar tingles through her. She knew this man. She was certain of it, even if she didn't remember him. It was merely a fleeting feeling, like the one she'd gotten from the man who had attacked her. Only, instead of registering Lawson as dangerous as she had her attacker, her instincts told her Lawson was safe.

She jerked away from him and gasped at her own realization. "I knew him. The man who attacked me. I knew him."

"You recognized him? Can you give me his name?"

"No, I don't know who he is. But I remember that when I saw him, I instinctively knew he was dangerous even before he grabbed the pillow and tried to smother me."

He sat on the bed and held her hand and Ashlee was thankful for his gentle touch—and his patience. She didn't need to be pushed.

"Do you think he did something to you, Ashlee? I mean before. Was he involved in whatever happened to you?"

She had no memory of what had led her to this situation, but her gut was telling her he was definitely involved. "I knew he was dangerous, so I must know him."

"Okay. You get some rest. We'll do everything we can to figure out who this guy is."

She wished she had more to give him—information that might actually help him *solve* this case tonight. She was being released tomorrow and while she'd be glad to be out of the hospital, the idea of a cold, empty hotel room frightened her. Surrounded by strangers with no idea who she could trust.

Why couldn't she remember?

"Thank you, Lawson."

He squeezed her hand, then stood.

"What happened between us?" she asked him before he could leave. He stopped, his shoulders slumped, then turned back to her.

"We can talk about that another time."

"No, please. I want to know. I get the feeling your brother doesn't care for me. Is it because of the engagement?" When he still hesitated, she barreled on. "Well, we obviously didn't get married, did we, or else you would have said I was your wife or your ex-wife. Instead, you said we were engaged. I assume we never made it to the altar."

He shook his head and walked back to the bed, pulling up the same stool his brother had sat on earlier. "Are you sure you want to hear this?"

So that meant she didn't turn out well in the story. Did she want to hear about what a horrible person she was? Not especially, no—but she still felt the need to learn everything she could about her past. Anything might be the puzzle piece that would help her understand who she was…and how she'd ended up here. "I do." She braced herself for the worst.

"We were engaged six years ago. We met in high school and dated exclusively after we graduated. I knew you had your doubts, not about me exactly, but about staying here in town, living on my family's ranch. It wasn't exactly your idea of a dream life."

That's funny because she thought living on a ranch sounded nice.

"Your grandparents had a ranch over on Cedar Ridge Road. That's where you lived with your parents and your sister, Bree, until about a year after your grandparents died. Your folks couldn't keep up with the ranch work and the bank foreclosed. When the rest of your family decided to move away from town, I thought for sure you would follow them. You always did have your sights set on the big city. But your parents settled in a retirement community, your sister moved to the city…and you stayed here with me. I thought it was a good sign. Truthfully, I realize now I ignored all the signs that you were unhappy."

She closed her eyes, knowing a painful thing was coming.

"The night before our wedding, you sent me a text message telling me you couldn't go through with it. By the time I reached your apartment, you were gone. I guess you probably sent that message once you were already miles away. You left me a letter taped to your door telling me all the reasons why we couldn't be together."

She closed her eyes, hating the pain that was evident in his face even now; the tightness of his mouth and jaw and the crease in his forehead as he recounted the events.

"I tried calling you and texting you, but you never replied. You were just gone. I even tried to find you. I was determined to be with you, Ashlee, no matter the cost. I wanted you and I resigned myself to living in the city if that was what it took." He looked away and hesitated. "But you never even gave me a chance. You shut me out. That was it. You were just gone."

Tears streamed from her eyes. That sense of familiarity that she'd gotten around him felt wrong now. She had no right to feel so safe around him when he had to be hurting just from being near her. She'd broken his heart. "I'm so sorry, Lawson. I'm sorry I did that to you."

"It was a long time ago."

He tried to shrug it away, like it didn't matter, but pain still flickered behind his eyes. It might have been a long time ago, but the hurt was still there and she was sure seeing her again had brought it all back up again.

"Still, I'm sorry. I wish I could remember and explain."

"There's no need. You made your choice. You didn't want to be here, so you left."

She didn't like the bitterness in his tone, but felt she deserved it. She'd treated him badly, broken his heart. Why was he even still here talking to her? He probably wanted answers from her, more answers that she didn't have to give.

He stood and took a deep breath. "So, you're right. My brother—my whole family—isn't too thrilled to hear you're back in town. But don't worry. It won't affect my or my brother's ability to do our jobs. We'll get to the bottom of what's happening to you."

She heard the underlying implication in his words. They wanted to find out what had happened to her and eliminate the danger so she could leave town again and they could resume their lives without her as a constant reminder of the pain she'd caused.

"Thank you for helping me, Lawson, and I am sorry. You seem like a nice guy. I hate that I hurt you."

"You didn't hurt me, Ashlee. You saved me from a life of misery." He headed for the door, obviously intent on leaving. But he stopped with his hand on the handle. "I'll be back in the morning when they discharge you. I'll drive you to the hotel. I'll also arrange to have security watch your room until I get here. Don't worry. You will be safe tonight. I promise."

He walked out and she struggled to process everything she'd just learned—everything she'd done in the past to hurt this kind, decent man. Her only contact in a town full of strangers and she'd already burned bridges with him. She pulled the covers over her head and let the tears flow.

She was truly all alone.

Lawson finished the chores for the evening, then saddled up his horse and took a ride. He needed time and space to think and process what had happened today. Ashlee was back in town. Seeing her again had done something to him—had opened up a deep hole in his soul.

He pushed the horse faster and faster as all the pain and grief and bitterness he'd been burying roared to the surface. For years, he'd pretended to have it all together, telling himself that he was over her. That he was past all the heartbreak and grief over what his life, their life together, could have been. All his plans and hopes for the future had been shattered in one person's selfish act.

The clouds above him rumbled as if imitating his heart and he slowed his horse, allowing them both to cool down from the brutal gallop. He felt like someone was chasing him, yet no matter how fast and hard he rode, he couldn't escape what was coming.

Thunder roared and the horse grew nervous at the oncoming storm, but Lawson wasn't ready to go back. He couldn't sit in that house and have his family watch him for signs that he was going off the edge again the way he had after his canceled wedding six years ago.

He knew he'd been a little crazy back then—pushing himself, taking too many risks to cover the pain he hadn't wanted to deal with. This land had healed him, brought him back to himself. His connection to this property was deep and he'd taken solace in the open ranges and grassy hills.

The rumbling sky opened up and rain poured down. Another round of thunder caused his mare to jerk again. He should have turned around and taken her back to the safety of the barn at the first hint of thunder, but he'd been selfish, needing to work out his own problems instead of thinking about her. Selfish. He'd been selfish with the horse just like he'd been selfish with Ashlee, putting his own wants and desires ahead of hers. He led the mare to a group of trees and slid off, tying her reins tightly around a limb so she couldn't bolt. They would be safe and dry here until the storm passed.

He stroked her nose to calm her and whispered to her that they were going to be all right. The horse, seemingly comforted by his tone and words, calmed down a bit.

He wished he could believe the assurances as easily as she did. He stretched out against a tree trunk and pulled a crumpled letter from his back pocket. The letter Ashlee had written to him and taped to her door six years ago. He'd read it and reread it a hundred times since that night and it still broke him.

Now she was back and all those old feelings were surfacing again. It wasn't right that he had to endure this pain again. It wasn't fair.

Why, God? Why are You doing this to me?

He stared up at the sky as the clouds began to clear and the storm passed.

His faith had always sustained him, but he was struggling now to make sense of this new trial. How was he ever going to be around her without giving in to the emotional roller coaster just seeing her had thrown him into? But he couldn't just leave her unprotected, could he? Why had he been the one to find her? And would it have made a difference if someone else had?

He didn't have all the answers, but he knew one thing. He couldn't abandon her. No matter what she'd done, no matter how badly she'd hurt him, he couldn't leave her alone and vulnerable, knowing someone was after her. He would have to figure out a way to be around her while still keeping his distance emotionally.

His family would tell him he was crazy for feeling so personally driven to help her, but his mama hadn't raised him to walk away from people in trouble. Ashlee needed his help and he would give it.

But he was trusting in God to help him keep his heart in check.

TWO

Lawson picked her up the next morning and drove her to the Sanderson Hotel. She opened her purse and pulled out her wallet. The picture on her driver's license stared back at her, mocking her struggles to recall anything about her life before yesterday. The image was definitely her, but the name seemed wrong. Ashlee Taylor. And the address was foreign to her. She didn't recall ever living at that address...or anywhere else for that matter.

Lawson pulled an overnight bag from the back of his pickup. "I hope you don't mind, but my mom sent over some of my sister Kellyanne's clothes."

"Won't she mind?"

"She's not in town. She keeps some things here, but she lives in Dallas. She's a social worker, so most of the clothes she leaves here are jeans and ranch outfits."

"Thank you. And please thank your mother for me."

She was grateful that they had thought about providing her with some clothes, otherwise she would have had to go out today to buy something. She still needed some personal supplies, but she wasn't up for shopping. She was too worn out—from the attack and from her inability to sleep last night for fear of the man who'd attacked her returning. How she'd wished for Lawson to be with her last night. But that was silly. He was her ex-fiancé. She'd run out on their wedding. He'd already been nicer to her than she deserved. She had no right to ask for anything more. She could make do on her own until she figured things out.

They went inside and checked in. Ashlee slipped a credit card from her wallet and handed it to the hotel clerk, hoping it would clear. For all she knew, her card was maxed out and her accounts empty. She would have to figure out how to find out that information, but that would mean recalling passwords and log-on information that were a complete mystery to her. Even answering the security questions banks always asked to recover account information would be difficult. Unless the information was her name or address or the name of her first love—she blushed thinking about that when she glanced up at him standing beside her—she wasn't getting into those accounts. Thankfully, the charge went through and the clerk handed her a plastic key card and told her she was in room 312.

Lawson walked her to the elevator, rode up with her, then opened the door and checked the room as she stood at the threshold.

"It's clear," he said.

She stepped inside. It looked like every other hotel room she'd ever heard of. A double bed in the center of the room, carpet on the floor, a TV on a dresser, and an attached bathroom. It wasn't much, but she realized she wasn't expecting much. Was she used to five-star hotels and restaurants? She didn't think so. This level of accommodation felt more her style—if she even had one.

"At some point, we'll need you to come down to the sheriff's office and give a statement, maybe look through some mug shots to see if we can identify the guy who attacked you."

"I'll try. But like I said, I don't remember much. It all happened so fast."

He nodded. "I didn't get a good look at him, either. No one did. Even the security footage isn't great. He was careful."

She leaned against the dresser. She'd also spent the night trying to come up with a scenario that would explain the bullet holes and the money. Had she stolen it from that man? Was she a thief? Was that her life? It didn't sound good. Somehow, she'd gotten into trouble with someone dangerous enough to try to kill her face-to-face. He'd tracked her to the hospital. Would he also track her to the hotel?

She shivered as she looked at her reflection and Lawson placed his hands on her shoulders. "It's going to be okay."

"Is it?" She glanced at him through the mirror over the dresser. "You don't know what's coming and neither do I. How do I know my attacker won't find me here?"

"We're increasing patrols around the hotel and security has been alerted. You'll be safe, Ashlee. Just lock the door and make sure you don't open it for anyone."

She was a prisoner in this room, she thought as she turned to face him, and she didn't even know why.

"I should go."

She wanted to ask him to stay, but that wasn't fair. She wasn't his problem and hadn't been since she'd walked out on him. Outside of the obligations of his job, it wasn't fair to expect him to help her. He'd already done so much.

"Thank you, Lawson." She kissed his cheek and he shuddered. She shouldn't have done that. It was too personal, too intimate, but he was all she knew, and she felt a pull toward him.

"I'll call you later to check on you."

He walked out and she locked the door behind him. She looked around the hotel room and shuddered. She didn't know what else to do now.

She opened the bag of food they'd picked up and ate, then stretched out on the bed. She needed rest. Maybe if she got some, her memory would return. But even when she turned out the lights and closed her eyes, her mind wouldn't quiet down. She kept mentally replaying the events of the past day and she couldn't make any sense of them. They were like a puzzle that needed putting together, but she was missing most of the pieces. If only she could remember!

Agitation bit through her and she jumped to her feet. Pacing felt more like her style. Her mind wasn't going to give up the necessary information, so she would just have to figure it out for herself.

She grabbed her purse and dumped it out on the bed. She opened her wallet. She had no cash in the billfold, so either she didn't carry any or everything she had was inside the duffel bag the police had confiscated.

She pulled out a ticket stub. A single ticket to a movie with a title she didn't recognize. Was she a movie buff?

Her wallet also contained several credit cards as well as business cards imprinted with her name. They were for an accounting firm called Brooke and Stephens. Could the danger she was facing have something to do with her work?

She picked up the phone and dialed the number on the card, but the call went straight to voice mail. It was odd hearing her own voice on the outgoing message, but she shook that off. At least she recognized it. She dialed zero and connected to an operator.

"Brooke and Stephens. How may I direct your call?"

Fear rustled through her. If this was all about something that had happened at her firm, should she be calling? Would she make things worse by contacting the people who might be targeting her? She decided she had to risk it for answers. "Hello? This is Ashlee Taylor."

"Good morning, Miss Taylor. How are you feeling?"

"I'm feeling fine. Thank you."

"Mr. Stephens told us he received a message from you saying you were sick and would be off for a few days."

So she'd made plans to be away from work. "I'm better, thank you. Is Mr. Stephens in the office? I'd like to speak to him."

"I'm sorry. He left for Las Vegas this morning for that conference. I'm sure you can contact him on his cell phone."

She didn't have that number and wasn't sure if she should ask. She had no clue what she was doing or even what she hoped to accomplish. "I seem to have lost his cell phone number…" She searched her memory for a name for the operator, but it didn't come.

"Anna," the girl replied.

"Of course. Anna, thank you. Can you give me that number?"

Anna recited the number and Ashlee hung up and dialed it before she lost her nerve. She still didn't know what she was going to say. Was she even close enough to this man to call him up?

"Hello?" a man's voice bellowed above loud background noise.

"Mr. Stephens? It's Ashlee Taylor."

"Ashlee! Is everything okay? Are you feeling better?"

"Not really. Something has happened and I need to ask you some questions."

"Hold on." The background noise softened as she waited for him to return to the call. "I had to leave the conference room. I could barely hear you. What's going on?"

She explained to him how she was back in her hometown with no memory of how she'd gotten there or why she'd come. "Do you have any idea what I was doing here? Did I say anything to you?"

"No, Ashlee. I'm sorry to say you didn't. The last time I saw you was when we were having dinner together. You left early, claiming you weren't feeling well. You've been working so hard so I assumed you were just worn down. I encouraged you to take some time to recharge. When you didn't show up for work the next day, I assumed you had taken my advice so I told everyone you were sick and were taking a few days off. Honey, are you okay? Do you need me to come pick you up? I can get a plane out in a few hours."

The intimacy of his tone surprised her. "Are we…? I'm sorry to have to ask this… but are we involved?"

Silence at her question told her the answer was yes.

"You've lost more than a few days, haven't

you? I should have known something was wrong when you called me Mr. Stephens when I answered the phone. What do you remember, Ashlee?"

She closed her eyes and tried again to push past the mental block in her mind. Nothing. "I don't remember anything. I don't remember you. I don't even remember me."

He took a few moments to process that, then answered. "We've been going out for a few months now."

"Is it serious?"

"I think so. Or at least, it's headed that way. I'm worried about you, Ashlee. I'll check the plane schedules and let you know when I'll be in town."

"No, you don't need to come." She couldn't imagine how Lawson would feel having her new boyfriend fly in. But why was Lawson her first concern rather than this man, whom she appeared to be dating? It was normal for him to be worried about her, wasn't it? Shouldn't she be pleased to have a boyfriend who clearly cared about her?

"I'm coming, Ashlee. Now, is this the number of the hotel where you're staying?"

"Yes." She gave him the hotel information including her room number.

"I'll see you soon." He hung up and she

wasn't certain if she was glad he was on his way or not.

She hated the feeling of uncertainty that had taken over her life. He could be feeding her a line when it came to his description of their relationship, but he had sounded concerned about her. She wished for a computer where she could look up the company and at least have an idea of what to expect. Her face warmed as she realized she didn't even know the man's first name!

The hotel probably had a business center where she could use the computer, but Lawson had told her to stay put.

She remained in place, anxious and still, until her need for information overrode her sense of fear.

She took the elevator downstairs and found the business center. They had two computers and both were available.

She keyed up the browser and typed in Brooke and Stephens. A web site popped up explaining that it was an accounting firm. She clicked through the employee list and found her photo. She was listed as an account manager. Nothing about her job description seemed familiar. She kept clicking through, hoping that someone's photo would trigger a memory. She finally found the photo of Stephens. His first name was Jake and he was a good-looking man, probably a few years older than she was. The web site listed him as a founding partner in the firm.

She tried to imagine this man putting his arms around her the way Lawson had. Nothing. No memories or sense of familiarity at all. It didn't make any sense to her that a man she hadn't seen in six years was more familiar to her than the man she was currently dating. But that might change when she actually saw Jake Stephens in person and not just as a photograph on a web site.

Ashlee checked her social media accounts next. She didn't know her log-on or password, but whoever had used the computer before her had failed to log out and she was able to use their account since she didn't seem to have any privacy locks on hers.

She was able to view photos of herself in her apartment, out with friends, posing with her cat—apparently named Mel. There was also a recent shot of her and her sister taken just last week, according to the date on the post. It was eerie to see her and her sister together. Lawson had said they were twins, but they were shockingly identical. Even their hairstyles were similar.

She wondered where Bree was and if she

was trying to reach her. She clicked on the link and wrote out a message for Bree to contact her at the hotel. She didn't go into details, only mentioned that something had happened and she needed to speak with her. Since she was using a stranger's account, she wished she had some inside knowledge to prove to Bree that it really was her, but those memories wouldn't come. She pressed Send and had no choice but to hope her sister would see it soon and respond.

She flipped through Bree's social media pages and found the same photo posted on the same day. But the other photos in her profile were of Bree with a man, and their poses were more intimate with captions like "Me and Travis" followed by several heart emojis.

Must be Bree's boyfriend—or maybe her ex?

The most current photo with Travis was dated over six months ago. It was possible they'd since broken up. Reaching out to him, too, might be a risk, but Ashlee decided to take the chance. She quickly typed a message to Travis with the same info and asked him to have Bree call her if he saw her. Then she hit Send. A sense of unease gripped her as she stared at the photos of Travis. She must not have liked her sister's boyfriend much, but hopefully, he could be of some help to her in reaching Bree.

Ashlee shut down the computer and returned upstairs to her room, securing the locks behind her. She hoped someone would reach out soon. She needed answers about what was happening in her life to have caused all of this. She needed to know. Lawson hadn't seen her in years, so he had no idea what she'd been doing. Ashlee could only hope that Bree would know, or maybe this Jake Stephens.

She took a shower and tried to wash away the fear and worry that had overtaken her since yesterday. She slipped into a hotel bathrobe and was towel drying her hair when she stepped out of the bathroom and someone grabbed her from behind.

She gasped as he pinned her arms behind her back with one hand and pressed a knife to her throat with the other. She glanced up. It was the same man who'd attacked her yesterday. "What...what do you want?"

"Where is it?"

Fear rustled through her. "Where is what?"

"The money! Where is the money?"

"The police took it. They have it. Please, please don't hurt me."

"If you don't have my money, then you're

no use to me anymore." He dug the knife into her throat and she screamed out as it sliced through her skin. But the blistering pain also pushed away the fear that had kept her paralyzed. In that moment, she knew one thing about herself with absolute certainty.

She wasn't the type of person to give up without a fight.

She headbutted him and he cried out. Ignoring the mix of blunt pain to the back of her head and the sharp jab from the knife's edge, she headbutted him again, then kicked and struggled until he stumbled backward and lost his balance. They both hit the floor and as the knife fell from her neck, she slipped out of his grip. He swore and reached out to grab her again, but not before she snatched a lamp from the nightstand and slammed it over his head.

Blood ran down his face and he'd dropped the knife—but he wasn't unconscious and he'd gotten back to his feet. She had to run.

Ashlee lunged for the door, turning the locks and rushing into the hallway. She reached the elevator just as it opened, and as she hurried inside, she saw her attacker stumbling out of her room. He spotted her and headed her way. If he reached her before the doors closed, she was dead, but she decided staying put was the best choice of action.

She was right. He reached the elevator just as the doors closed.

She nearly doubled over in relief at the near miss, but reminded herself that she wasn't safe yet. He would still be after her. He was probably rushing down the stairs to meet her at the bottom and she willed the elevator to go faster. When it stopped and the doors slid open, she crept to the opening and scanned the lobby and the people milling about. He wasn't anywhere in sight. She had no idea where he was, but surely he wouldn't be brazen enough to come after her with all these witnesses.

She bolted for the front desk and the clerk on duty. "Help me! I need help." Adrenaline fading, her legs gave out and she crumpled to the floor as the desk clerk rushed around to help her.

Two attacks in two days.

And she was all alone.

Lawson received the call from Cecile about the attack. Immediately, he jumped into his truck and headed for the hotel. He knew he should just let Cecile handle it, but he had to make certain for himself that Ashlee was all right.

He reached the hotel and found her huddled in a chair in the manager's office, her white robe covered in blood and Kyle Deaver, a two-year veteran of the sheriff's office, standing watch over her.

Kyle spotted him and turned to Ashlee. "I'll go call Cecile and let her know Lawson is here."

"Thank you, Deputy Deaver," she said, giving him a forced smile of gratitude.

Lawson thanked him, too, then took the chair beside Ashlee, reaching for her hand. It was still trembling with fear. "What happened?"

"A man. He was in my room when I got out of the shower. He put a knife to my neck."

He spotted the bandage where she'd been cut. That accounted for the blood on her bathrobe. "Did he say what he wanted?"

She put her hand over her mouth as if holding in tears before she answered him. "He wanted the money. He said it belonged to him. What does that mean? Did I steal it?"

That made no sense to him. The Ashlee he knew wasn't a thief. But he forced himself to acknowledge that he didn't really know her anymore. "Have the paramedics been here?"

"Cecile called them, but I refused to go back to the hospital. They just left."

"You should get checked out."

"I'm fine. He cut my neck, but it's not deep. I don't want to spend another night in the hospital. I don't need to."

The elevator dinged and Cecile stepped out carrying the suitcase Lawson had brought for Ashlee when she'd checked into the hotel.

Lawson and Ashlee both stood to meet her. "I thought you might need this," Cecile said, handing over the case. "I noticed you hadn't unpacked and I figured you could use a change of clothes. Plus, I'm going to need that robe for evidence."

Ashlee glanced down at the red stains on the robe. "I'll run into the bathroom to change." She hurried into the attached bathroom and closed the door.

Lawson turned to Cecile. "Did you find anything?"

She nodded as he took his seat again. "Blood on the lamp and the floor from where she hit him. We'll run it for DNA to see if we have any matches. We're also fingerprinting the room, but it's a hotel, so getting a good lead with fingerprints will be tough."

He hated to think this guy might get away clean again. When Ashlee returned, now dressed in a pair of jeans and one of his sister's button-up shirts, he had more questions for her. "How did he get into your room? Were the doors locked?"

"Yes, I locked them. I even had the bolt latched—I'm sure of it because I had to unlatch it when I ran out. He must have gotten in when I came downstairs to the business center."

Irritation bit at him. He'd told her to stay locked inside her room and she'd done just the opposite...just like she always had. "Why did you do that?"

"I found my business card in my wallet. I wanted to look up the company, see if it would trigger any memories. I also spoke to my boss and found out I'd taken time off from work."

"Was he able to tell you about anything dangerous you might have gotten into?" Cecile asked her, cutting off any further questions Lawson was going to ask. She shot him a glance that told him plainly that now was not the time to chastise her, but to get answers.

She was right, of course, and he was glad she was the one assigned to Ashlee's case.

Ashlee shook her head. "No, he really believed I was sick. He's getting on a plane to come here as soon as he can."

That struck Lawson as odd. "Why is your boss coming here?"

"Because apparently he's also my boyfriend. We've been dating a few months."

Her words rocked him like a punch to the gut and nearly sent him to his knees. Her boyfriend was coming here. Someone she would rather be with than him. He stood and tried to regain his bearings after that blow. He didn't want to know this man and he didn't like the idea of his arrival, but it was right that the man do so, wasn't it? He was her life now, not Lawson. He had more reason to worry about her than a six-years-past ex did.

"At least we know the money is in play. This guy was after it. Did you tell him the police have it?"

Ashlee nodded. "I told him. He said he had no more use for me then. That was when he tried to slit my throat."

Lawson shuddered at how cold that sounded. His blood was boiling at the idea that someone had placed a knife to her throat and was ready to use it to kill her. And if the attacker's behavior at the hospital was any indication, he wouldn't have hesitated, either. She'd survived because she'd fought back.

But what if her efforts hadn't been enough? This man was strong. Determined. And lethal. She'd become a target of a killer's wrath.

Cecile took out her phone. "I'm going to call the evidence room to alert them in case this guy decides to try to retrieve his money."

"When can I go back to my room?" Ashlee asked Cecile.

"We're still processing the scene. It may be a while. I'm sure the hotel can arrange for another room for you."

Lawson glanced around, astounded at the lack of security in the place. How could he have left her here unguarded? He'd mistakenly believed she would be safe with the locks and the increased patrols and the security staff. He would have a conversation with the management later.

Still, it was clear to him that she wasn't safe here. This guy knew where to find her and she was a sitting target in this hotel. Somehow, her assailant had tracked her, possibly by the use of her credit card—or maybe he'd followed them from the hospital. Whatever the case, she couldn't stay here and she wouldn't be any safer in another hotel. It would only be a matter of time before he tracked her there, too.

Lawson realized they were playing a race

against time game. Could this guy get to her before she regained her memory?

But how could she work her way through amnesia when she was under so much stress, in sterile, impersonal environments? She needed to be someplace familiar where something might spark her memory. Plus, the closer she was, the easier it would be to keep her safe.

"I think you should come stay with us at the ranch."

Both Ashlee and Cecile turned to stare at him. Ashlee protested first. "I don't know."

"Look, I know it's not the place you want to be, but it's secure and no one will find you there. My brothers are in town, so they'll be around to help protect you. Plus, it's a familiar place. You were there a lot once upon a time. Maybe it will help to spark something."

Cecile gave a resigned sigh. "Much as I hate to admit it, I think it's a good idea. With your brothers in town, plus you and Josh and your dad, it's probably the safest place in town for Ashlee."

He saw the look of concern on Cecile's face. She and Josh had been friends for years. She knew the history with Ashlee and knew Josh, always the overprotective brother, would not be happy with Lawson's suggestion. But it was Lawson's home, too. In fact, he handled most of the day-to-day operations of the ranch. He had a right to bring whomever he liked to stay there.

"I'll tell Josh. You finish up here." He glanced at Ashlee and hated the hesitation he saw on her face. She couldn't even remember him or their past, yet her dislike for the ranch was clearly evident with or without her memories.

"I don't want to be a burden," she said.

"You won't be." He steeled himself against the rejection in her tone for the place he loved so dearly. He consoled himself that she couldn't remember how much his family's homestead meant to him. She wasn't intentionally putting him down. But Silver Star was in his blood. It had been in his family for six generations and he was thankful to be able to call it his own and work the land every day. He'd never wanted anything else in his life...except for Ashlee. But he hadn't realized he couldn't have them both. That had been his downfall.

She finally gave in. "Okay, I'll go."

He walked her outside to his truck, but he didn't get right in. First, he had to alert Josh and the rest of his family that he was bringing her. He didn't want to blindside them.

He made the call, got in behind the wheel, then stopped by a local pharmacy to let Ashlee pick up a few necessities. On the way home, he drove around for a while, taking the back roads and watching his mirrors, making certain they weren't being followed.

The danger she was in had him worried, but he told himself everything would be fine. There was no way anyone would connect her to the ranch. She hadn't been a part of their lives in a long time. She would be safe.

He was far less certain about the safety of his heart.

THREE

Lawson pulled off the main road, guiding them under the ranch gate entry sign that read Silver Star Ranch. Ashlee glanced out the window and took in the grass fields and trees for as far as she could see. The area seemed like a beautiful place to grow up and she wished she remembered more of it—or why she'd left.

"This is your family's place?"

"Yep. Silver Star Ranch has been in my family for six generations."

She liked the idea of stability. Something about that kind of history appealed to her. "That's nice."

He grimaced, but remained silent.

"What?" she insisted.

"You didn't used to think so. You thought I was foolish for wanting to stay here. You called me unambitious, but all I ever wanted was to run this ranch and start a family with you, Ash."

Her face flushed with embarrassment. How could she have run out on this good-looking guy who seemed to have loved her so much? Even with an addled brain, she knew she must have been crazy.

"I'm sorry. I wish I could explain."

"I wish you could, too. I wish you had talked to me instead of running away, Ashlee."

Again, her face burned with embarrassment. "You're judging me on something I don't remember doing."

"I'm sorry. You're right. This isn't a re-union—not for you, anyway. You've been through something terrible and I need to remember that. I didn't mean to make this an inquisition. No more talk about the past. I promise."

She turned away and watched the land-scape flowing by instead. No point in talking about something she didn't even remember. Besides, she apparently had more important things going on in her life than once having broken the heart of Lawson Avery.

He parked in front of a beautiful white farmhouse with a wraparound porch. She got out and looked around, noting a vegetable garden on the side of the house and a large barn close by. Everything about this place was lovely and welcoming, and she felt instantly at home here.

And safe. She felt safe here.

Lawson walked up beside her, the suitcase in his hand. "I called ahead to let everyone know what was happening with you so they wouldn't be surprised to see you. They know you don't remember them."

She recalled Josh's earlier reaction to her and braced herself, trying to remember she had a history with these people that she couldn't recall. "How many brothers do you have?" she asked as they stepped onto the porch.

"Four brothers and a sister, but Kellyanne returned to Dallas yesterday. My brothers, Colby and Miles, are still here. They'll be leaving in a few days—but while they're here, you can trust them to keep you safe. Colby's an FBI agent and Miles is a US Marshal."

She knew about Josh, but that still left one brother unaccounted for. "With Josh, that's only four kids."

"Paul is Special Forces. He was injured in a SEALs' combat mission several months ago. He's staying here while he recuperates."

He opened the front door and led her inside. His family greeted her cordially, but she felt their stares, their silent judgments. She'd hurt someone they cared about, and they held a grudge. She couldn't blame them for that.

"I'm Diane Avery," a woman said, stepping forward to take her hand. "Lawson's mother. It's good to see you again, Ashlee."

"It's nice to see you."

Lawson pointed out four men who'd stood to greet her. "You met my brother Josh at the hospital. These are my other brothers, Colby, Miles and Paul, and that's my father, Marshall."

"It's nice to see you all." She purposely didn't say it was nice to meet them since, apparently, she had already met them all before. She'd nearly been a part of this family, but she'd run off instead. It didn't make sense to her. But it must be true, and not just because she didn't believe Lawson would lie about something like that. There was something familiar about this house and the warmth of it. She'd been here before—had felt happy and safe. She could only hope that she might someday feel that way again.

"I'll show you where you can stay," Diane told her.

Lawson handed her the suitcase, then nodded her on. "I'll check on you soon."

She followed Diane upstairs to a room at the end of the hallway. A terrible feeling of guilt washed over her, like she'd done something wrong and shouldn't be here. Well, yes…she'd run out on her wedding like a scared little girl.

Diane opened a door for her and led her into a nicely antique-furnished room. It was simple, but clean and fresh.

"Mrs. Avery, I hope you don't mind my staying here. I don't want to be an inconvenience."

"Nonsense. You're welcome."

"Am I? Even after what I did?"

"I was under the impression you didn't remember anything."

"No, I don't remember. Lawson told me. I can't offer you an explanation, but—"

Diane reached out to her. "It's water under the bridge, Ashlee."

Angry raised voices floated up from the den to belie her assurance. Ashlee heard her name mentioned more than once and knew Lawson's brothers were not as willing to be as welcoming as his mother.

Diane closed the bedroom door. "Never mind that. All my boys can be hotheaded, but any one of them would have done the same thing in bringing you here, given the situation. For right now, let's focus on you getting your memory back and keeping you safe." She opened the closet and took out a thick blanket for the bed. "This is my daughter's bedroom when she's home. I sent you several things she had here, but there might be a few more pairs of jeans and some shirts and boots in the closet. Help yourself to whatever you can find."

She left Ashlee alone and when the door closed Ashlee fell onto the bed and sighed. Was this the right thing to do? To be in this house knowing how she'd hurt Lawson? Part of her felt that she should leave. But on the other hand, she didn't have a lot of choices.

Ugh! If only she could remember!

She pressed her hands against her forehead and tried to push past the mental block in her mind, but nothing would come. She didn't recall being shot at or why she'd come back to this town. She didn't remember anything about her past. Her mother? Her father? The only family that seemed familiar was her sister, and that was just because she shared the same face. Who else in her life was she close to?

Ashlee glanced at her finger and saw no wedding ring. She wasn't married. No, she wouldn't be, not if she was dating Jake Stephens.

But someone was out there looking for her, looking to kill her.

A chill ran up her spine and she picked up the blanket and wrapped it around her shoulders.

Was the doctor right? Had something so terrible happened to her that she'd blocked it from her memory? What could that have been?

And did she really want to recall it?

"I can't believe you brought her back here," Colby said. His tone was angry and bitter, and although Lawson knew the fury was on his behalf, he didn't care for it.

"She's in trouble. She needs help."

"But it doesn't have to be from you," Paul stated.

"I know, but I should help her. I can't let our past dictate how I treat her. She's in a vulnerable state."

"So true," his mother said, descending the stairs and joining the conversation. "Hate doesn't solve anything."

"We're not talking about hate, Mom," Miles said. "We're talking about boundaries. Little brother here doesn't seem to have them."

"I loved her once. I just don't want to see anything bad happen to her. That's all."

Some days he was glad to have his brothers home on leave from their duties. Today was not one of those days. While he was glad to have plenty of trained, capable protectors at hand, if he could have brought Ashlee home without their audience, he would have preferred it.

"I have some work to do in the barn," Paul said, grabbing his hat and gloves and limping out. He'd suffered both physical and emotional injuries during his last mission with the Navy SEALs and the physical work of the ranch helped to soothe his frayed nerves.

Colby and Miles each grabbed their hats and followed Paul through the door.

"Thanks for understanding, Mom," Lawson said as his brothers went off on their own ways.

She glanced around the empty room. "Where is your father? He was here when I went upstairs."

"He said he was feeling tired and needed a nap. Actually, I think he was just trying to stay out of the lecture he knew my brothers were going to give me."

"I'll check on him in a minute. First, I want to fix Ashlee something to eat. It's several hours until supper and she might need something to tide her over." She hurried into the kitchen and busied herself preparing a sandwich. "You did the right thing," she said when he entered the kitchen. "With her family gone from here, she has no one left to look out for her. Bringing her to Silver Star was the right decision."

"I'm glad at least one person doesn't think I've lost my mind."

She stopped and looked up at him, worry creasing her face. "I said it was the right decision. I didn't say it was a good one. When I think of what that girl put you through…" She shook her head, then sighed and turned back to her task of sandwich making. "I've prayed for that girl again and again. I just never thought God would see fit to bring her back to Silver Star."

He understood her concern. Losing Ashlee six years ago had sent him to a dark place. It made sense that his mother—along with the rest of his family—was worried he might go there again. He worried about that, too, but he was determined to help her without involving his heart. "I never thought He would, either, but I can't just abandon her, can I?"

"No, you can't. None of us can. I just worry what she's gotten herself into."

"Me, too. All that money, the bullet holes, amnesia. The doctor said she must have witnessed something traumatic to trigger the memory loss. I can believe it."

He'd seen terrible things in his time as a deputy and the stories his brothers told often shocked and horrified him. He hated to think about all the terrible things that could have happened to Ashlee. He didn't want to know the truth, but they would both have to face it to figure out what kind of danger she'd gotten herself into.

The family was courteous and polite, but Ashlee felt the underlying tension as she sat at the large family table for supper. All the brothers were present, including Josh, who'd arrived at the house sometime while she was still upstairs. The table was filled with dishes of roast beef, potatoes, green beans and rolls, and everything smelled wonderful.

Lawson had shown her where to sit, then taken the chair beside her. She was glad he was nearby because she felt like she was navigating strange and hostile waters being in this house surrounded by his parents and his brothers.

Marshall Avery bowed his head and everyone else followed suit. Lawson reached for her hand and she gave it, joining hands with Diane on the other side. Marshall quickly spoke the blessing, then everyone dug in.

Ashlee filled her plate sparingly, but her appetite wasn't what it should have been and she knew she couldn't finish even what she'd taken.

Conversation at the table changed rapidly, ranging from Lawson's description of a mare about to give birth to Colby readying to take on a new FBI assignment to Josh's turning back to Ashlee's case.

"Cecile and I were discussing going to Dallas to check out your apartment," Josh said. "There might be a clue there."

She nodded. "That sounds like a good idea."

"We'll go," Lawson volunteered. "We can drive up tomorrow."

Once that was settled, they moved on to another conversation about someone in town whose farm was at risk of foreclosure. They all lamented how commonplace such a thing was becoming.

"We've been blessed," Marshall stated. "We've had some close calls, but God has always pulled us out of hot water."

Lawson nodded. "I pray He always will."

Supper ended and Ashlee offered to help with the dishes. She was quickly shooed away by Diane, who insisted the boys always cleaned up after a big meal.

She walked into the den and stared at the photos displayed on the wall. Miles in his official US Marshals' photo. Colby receiving his FBI credentials. Paul's military picture was next to Kellyanne's and Lawson's graduation photos. They looked like a nice, caring family.

Ashlee spotted Lawson when he came out of the kitchen and pointed to the photos. "Your parents must be so proud of you all," she commented.

"Yes, they are."

She motioned toward the photo of a dark-haired girl. "Your sister is very pretty."

"She's tough, too. She had to be to grow up with five brothers." When she'd finished examining the pictures, he walked her upstairs to her room and talked about going to her apartment the next day. "We should get an early start. It's a three-hour drive from here."

"I'll be up," she said, certain she wouldn't be able to sleep. She was suddenly very anxious to see her place and hopefully get some answers.

She went to bed and tried to imagine her apartment, but even that wouldn't come except for the images she'd briefly seen while checking out her social media pages.

It was unnerving and she was thankful when morning finally arrived and she and Lawson were on the road.

They rode in an easy silence, the music from the radio filling the cab of the truck for most of the ride. The hours flew by until he pulled into her apartment complex. She took out the key Cecile had given her from her purse. She wouldn't have even known which apartment was hers except for the address listed on her license and vehicle registration. The apartment complex was small and all the units faced a courtyard. Apartment 6B was on the second floor, so they took the stairs. She sucked in a breath as she inserted the key into the lock. She glanced at Lawson who nodded, assuring her that he was ready for whatever awaited them. It suddenly occurred to her that she didn't know if she had any form of security system and she wouldn't know the pass code if she did. Oh well, they would deal with that if and when it came up.

She turned the key and pushed open the door. Inside, the living room had been ransacked. Lawson pulled his weapon, then pushed past her and took in the scene. He checked the bedrooms and bathroom and announced the apartment was clear of people.

She couldn't get much of a sense of the décor amid all the mess and yet...nothing seemed familiar to her. Not the furniture or the appliances. She picked up a photograph of her and her sister, the same one she'd seen on social media. Even that was unfamiliar.

"Any idea what happened here?" Lawson asked.

She shook her head. "Not a clue." Nothing was coming back to her. This might as well have been someone else's wreck of an apartment.

Ashlee stepped into one of the bedrooms and noted it had also been trashed. "Why would someone do this?"

He shrugged. "If I had to guess, I'd say they were searching for the money."

That made sense. Her apartment would have been the first place they would have looked. It hadn't been here, of course, because she'd had it with her in the car.

"Hello?" The voice from the doorway was soft and questioning, and just a little brittle.

Lawson spun and raised his gun and Ashlee's heart jumped at the noise. He quickly lowered his weapon when he spotted an elderly lady, holding a cat, standing in her doorway.

"Hello?" Ashlee responded.

The woman glanced around with concern at the mess. "What happened here?"

"We're not sure," Lawson stated.

She gave Ashlee a questioning look. "Bree?"

And suddenly her confusion made sense. She was just trying to figure out who she was talking to—if she was a neighbor, then she probably would have expected Ashlee to call her by name, or at least show some sign of recognition. "I'm Ashlee."

Lawson holstered his gun as the woman entered.

"Have you seen anyone coming or going out of here?" Ashlee asked.

"No, I haven't. Not since I saw you rush out two days ago. But I found Mel. He was wandering. He must have run out when you left."

"Or when someone broke in and trashed the place," Lawson suggested.

The woman held out the cat and Ashlee reached to take it. The large tabby purred and rubbed against her and Ashlee found it comforting to have him in her arms, all the more so from the familiar feeling it gave her.

"Thank you for returning him, Mrs....?"

She glanced at Ashlee, confused. "McAlpin."

"I'm sorry, Mrs. McAlpin. Everything is just a little bit confusing right now."

"I hope your sister is okay."

Ashlee glanced at Lawson, then back at the woman. "Do you have reason to think she wouldn't be?" So far, Bree hadn't reached out to her. She'd left her contact info at the hotel in the message she'd sent Bree, but when she'd moved to the ranch, she'd asked the hotel manager to alert her through the sheriff's office if her sister phoned. So far, she'd heard nothing.

"I just haven't seen either of you in several days."

"So my sister was staying here with me?"

"Yes, she's been staying here for several months now. Why are you asking all these questions?"

"I have to be honest, Mrs. McAlpin. I was in an accident and I'm having trouble remembering things."

Mrs. McAlpin gasped and reached out a concerned hand to Ashlee. "Are you all right?"

"I'm fine except I haven't been able to reach my sister and I'm worried about her."

"I haven't seen her, either, but I hope she's all right. She's been trying so hard to get her life together."

"Has she?" Lawson asked. "In what way?"

"Well, I know Ashlee has been concerned about her for a long time now. She fell in with the wrong crowd and took up with a man who was into drugs. She finally came to her senses and decided she wanted something better for herself, so she left him and moved in here with Ashlee." She glanced at Ashlee. "You were so excited when she did. You told me you felt like you'd finally gotten your sister back."

She smiled, wishing she could recall that tender moment. Still, it was nice to hear.

Lawson took a business card from his pocket and handed it to the woman. "If you notice anyone return here, or spot anyone suspicious hanging around, call this number. We'd especially like to talk to Bree to let her know what's happened to Ashlee, so please pass this number along to her if you see her."

"You're not staying?" she asked Ashlee.

"I don't think it's a good idea at the moment. It may not be safe for me to be back here for now."

"Would you like me to keep Mel for you until you return?"

Ashlee hated the idea of leaving him behind, but it felt wrong to take him to someplace he wasn't familiar with just to make herself feel better. Besides, she already felt like enough of an imposition. "Would you mind?"

"Certainly not. I've enjoyed having him around for the past few days."

Ashlee handed the cat back to Mrs. McAlpin and said her goodbyes. She hoped she would hear from her soon with news that Bree had returned to the apartment. She turned and looked around at the mess of her ransacked home and a terrible thought hit her. "You don't think Bree was here when whoever broke in did this, do you?"

He glanced around and even though she could see he wanted to reassure her, he couldn't do it. Perhaps that was why her sister wasn't responding to her messages. She shuddered at the thought—especially when a new realization struck her. If someone was trying to kill her, might they accidentally mistake her sister for her?

She crossed her arms and tried to rub away the unshakable dread that flowed through her that something terrible had happened to her sister and it was all because of her.

Lawson saw her fear and pulled her into a gentle embrace. "She might not have been here. There's no blood on the floor and no obvious signs of a struggle. It looks to me that whoever did this was looking for the money."

She wiped away a single tear that slid down her cheek and prayed he was right. If anything happened to Bree because of her, she would never forgive herself.

"While I'm here, I may as well grab some of my clothes." She walked into the bedroom and packed some things into a suitcase, taking the opportunity while he wasn't hovering over her to pull herself together. She wouldn't get through this, wouldn't find her sister, by falling apart.

Lawson carried the case to the truck. As they pulled away from the parking lot, she stared at the apartment and wondered how long it would be before she could return to her normal life, or even what normal was to her.

"Tell me about my sister," Ashlee asked after they'd been on the road for a while. She noticed him hesitate, but she was determined to know. "Please. You can't imagine how awful it is not to know anything about your identical twin sister. What is she like?"

"I'm not sure what you mean."

"Is she the type of person to disappear without answering my calls or messages? Mrs. McAlpin mentioned she was trying to get her life back together. Do you have any idea what that means?"

He grimaced, and her stomach sank. For him to be this reluctant...she could only assume that meant he didn't think she'd like what he had to say. He obviously didn't want to bad-mouth her sister, but she deserved to know the truth.

Finally, he spoke. "I haven't seen or heard from her in years... But when we were in school, and even after, word got around that she'd started hanging around with the wrong type of people."

"Type of people?"

"People who were into drinking, drugs, theft. I hope for your sake that what Mrs. McAlpin said is true and she is trying to make a better life for herself. She was always hanging around with the troublemakers and pulling you down with her. I remember a week before our wedding, you had to drive to Dallas to bail her out of jail. I begged you to let her sit there and face the consequences of her actions, but you refused. She called and you rushed to help her."

Ashlee bristled at his harsh tone. "It doesn't sound like you like her very much."

"Like I said, I haven't seen her in years. I just hope what's happening isn't because of her—that she hasn't pulled you into another one of her messes."

She hadn't even considered that this might be her *sister's* mess that she was caught up in. If that was the case, then perhaps Bree was in serious trouble. If Ashlee had escaped with bullets being fired at her car, what was Bree having to endure? But surely Ashlee wouldn't have left Bree behind. That didn't make sense to her, either.

She noticed Lawson tense and speed up. "What's the matter?"

"A car's approaching from behind us."

She glanced back and spotted a car closing in on them. *Please just let it pass by.* But it didn't. It slowed and someone leaned out from the window with a gun aimed at them.

"Hang on," Lawson said, hitting the accelerator and speeding away.

The man in the car started firing and Ashlee screamed.

"Get down," he said, pushing her head toward her knees.

Another shot rang out. Lawson reached for his cell phone and hit a button. It started ringing and moments later, Josh's voice came on the line.

"We're on the highway just outside of town. Someone in a car is shooting at us. It's a blue sedan, maybe a Taurus or similar make. One driver. One shooter—"

Another shot rang out and the truck veered. "He hit the tire," Lawson said as he fought for control. "I can't hold it on the road."

Ashlee screamed as the truck flipped and rolled down the ravine, each tumble jolting her as glass broke and metal crunched. They hit the bottom and the air bag deployed, forcing her head to slam against the seat. Stars played against her eyes and her whole world went topsy-turvy before the spinning turned to nothingness and she blacked out.

Lawson groaned as something wet and sticky dripped down his face. He touched his head and felt blood against his fingers. He started to check his head in the mirror, then realized the mirror wasn't there any longer. The truck was on its side and he was only staying in position because of his seat belt.

He clicked it off, then struggled to regain his bearings.

Ashlee.

He looked over and found her unconscious, slumped against her seat. He unbuckled the seat belt and let her fall into his arms. She seemed uninjured, but he couldn't be sure until she awoke. He gently patted her cheeks. "Ashlee. Ashlee, can you hear me?"

Her eyes began to flutter and she opened one, then the other. "What happened?"

"We ran off the road and flipped. Are you okay?"

"I think so." She touched her forehead, then glanced at him and gasped. "You're bleeding."

"It's only a gash, I think. It won't kill me." But whoever had shot out his tires would be more than happy to finish the job if they came looking. "We need to get out of here." He searched the debris for his cell phone and found the screen busted. He tried to bring it to life, but it was dead. At least he'd been on the line with his brother when the men had attacked, and he'd been able to give their location. He knew Josh would send help. They just had to survive until the cavalry arrived.

He helped Ashlee crawl out from the truck. They were both rattled from the shock of the crash, but they didn't have time to stop and process—they had to take cover in case those men came to make certain they'd died.

He pushed her into the woods and took cover behind a tree. His head was pounding and blood was sliding into his field of vision. Head wounds were notorious for bleeding, so he wasn't worried about the injury, but he would have to see about it soon.

If he was still alive to do so.

He heard rustling in the distance and motioned for Ashlee to be quiet. He glanced out and heard voices and movement as someone came down the embankment. Two figures appeared, guns in hand, and approached the truck, searching inside.

"They're gone," one of them said.

The other noticed the blood. "They can't have gotten far. Let's finish this."

Lawson flinched as the gunmen headed toward them, but then stopped as sirens wailed in the distance.

"Let's get out of here," one man shouted. The other man agreed and followed him up the embankment.

Lawson heard the squeal of tires as they roared away. He hurried to the edge of the embankment and spotted two cruisers screech to a halt. *Thank You, Lord, for Josh's quick response.*

He owed his brother for arriving in the nick of time.

Josh appeared at the top of the embankment, obviously surveying the overturned truck. "Is either of you injured?"

"We're okay," Lawson shouted up to him. "Just shaken up."

Josh and another deputy helped them up the hill and into a waiting ambulance. As expected, his gash wasn't deep, but did need a few stitches. He watched as a paramedic checked Ashlee over. He knew she wasn't injured from the crash. They'd both been fortunate. The accident could have been much worse.

But his concern for her was heightened. Men out there still wanted her dead. But who and why?

FOUR

Every inch of her body ached after the crash, but Ashlee refused to go back to the hospital. She sat in the waiting area of the sheriff's office, a blanket draped over her shoulders, nursing a cup of water as Lawson, Josh and Cecile went over the details of the accident in the conference room behind her.

Terror shuddered through her at how close they'd been to another deadly confrontation with the men who'd run them off the road. Their demeanors had been cold and emotionless as they'd spoken about finishing this. Finishing *her*, they'd meant.

The sheriff's office door opened and a man entered, whistling an easygoing tune. It struck Ashlee as odd in the tension-filled office. He glanced into the conference room, then stopped at Deputy Deaver's desk. "I'm supposed to have a meeting with the sheriff, but he looks engaged in something else."

Deaver leaned back in his seat. "He sure is, Mr. Mayor. His brother was just run off the road and nearly killed."

"Really? Which brother?"

"Lawson."

"I hope he wasn't injured too badly."

"No, sir. Just shook up as far as I can tell."

The mayor turned and looked at Ashlee. She squirmed under his gaze, but he pasted a big smile on his face as he approached her. Before he could speak, the conference room door opened and Josh, Lawson and Cecile exited.

Josh approached the man. "I haven't forgotten about our meeting, Don, but we've got an urgent situation here. Can we reschedule?"

The mayor gave him a broad smile. "Of course. I hope everything is okay. Deputy Deaver told me about you being run off the road, Lawson. You're not hurt, I hope."

"No, Mayor. We're both fine."

"Both? There were two of you?"

"This is Ashlee Taylor. She's an old friend of mine." Lawson pointed to Ashlee and the mayor turned his gaze back to her.

He extended his hand. "Mayor Don Baxter. Nice to meet you."

She shook his hand. "Ashlee Taylor."

"Are you from these parts, Miss Taylor?"

"Yes, but I…" She was afraid the mayor would ask something about where she'd gone to school, or if she knew various people in town—questions she wouldn't be able to answer.

"It seems she's suffering from a bout of amnesia," Cecile interjected.

The mayor's eyes widened in surprise. "Really? I've never met anyone with amnesia. How much of your memory is missing?"

"All of it. I can't remember anything from before Lawson found me in my car. I didn't even know my name until he told me."

"That must be quite disconcerting for you."

Ashlee nodded. "Yes, it is. I wish I understood what was going on."

"The men who ran us off the road, they were after her," Lawson explained.

"That's terrible. Any leads as to who is behind these attacks?"

Lawson answered. "Nothing yet, but we're still gathering information. We'll figure it out."

"Well, I'll let you all get back to work. I hope everything turns out well for you, Miss Taylor."

"Thank you," Ashlee said.

He started to walk out, then turned back to Josh. "Oh, there was one thing I wanted to alert you about. I'm sure you've heard about that biker gang that has taken up residence at the Waveland Motel on the outskirts of town?"

Josh nodded. "We've received a few noise complaints about them, but no behavior that's reached a criminal level."

"Yes, well, I heard from a friend at Dallas PD that the feds are opening an investigation into the group for operating a counterfeiting ring. We can probably expect some federal agents to arrive in town any day now."

"Thanks for the heads-up. We'll keep an eye on them until they do."

When the mayor left, Josh looked at Cecile. "Get in touch with the Secret Service and double-check the serial numbers on the bills we found in Ashlee's car."

Lawson turned to face him. "You think Ashlee is involved with this gang?"

Cecile answered instead. "She does work for an accounting firm, and I've heard these groups often hire companies to manage their money. Apparently, it's a very lucrative lifestyle. I'm only speculating, but if she handled their accounts, she could have found evidence of counterfeiting and possibly taken the money to prove it."

"If they are counterfeit," Josh interjected,

"at least we'll know we're looking in the right direction. If not, then we'll move on to other leads. For now, we've posted a BOLO on the car that ran you off the road and I've got deputies canvasing the area looking for any witnesses. Your truck is pretty banged up, Lawson. I'm having it towed to Mike Morgan's place." He pulled a set of keys from his pocket and tossed them to Lawson. "You can use mine until it's fixed."

"Thank you."

Cecile held out a tablet to Ashlee. "I compiled a list of photos while Lawson was giving his statement. It's of known offenders in the system. I'd like for you both to go through them to see if you can identify the two men who ran you off the road and also the man who attacked you at the hospital and hotel. Do you think you can do that?"

"I'll never forget those men's faces," Ashlee said. She hadn't recognized the men who had run them off the road, but neither had been the man who'd previously attacked her. Both she and Lawson had gotten a good look at the ones from the car when they'd hidden from them in the woods. They hadn't bothered to disguise their faces, either, obviously unafraid of being recognized because they'd had no intention of leaving any witnesses alive.

So far, these men plus the man from the hotel and hospital were the only connections she had to whatever had happened to her. It was obvious this wasn't merely a case where she'd wronged one man. She'd come afoul of a group...possibly the biker gang the mayor had just warned them about.

Josh and Cecile left them alone and Ashlee turned to Lawson. "You don't really believe I'm involved with a biker gang, do you?" She shuddered at the thought of associating with a gang of any kind.

"I don't want to, but it's a lead we need to check out. Cecile told me and Josh earlier in the conference room that she's been through your financials and hasn't found anything out of the ordinary. That money didn't come from your accounts, which means you got it from somewhere else."

She sighed and rubbed a sore muscle on her neck. "I wish I could remember."

"Maybe we'll catch a break with these pictures." Lawson switched on the tablet and began scrolling through photos. He positioned the screen where they could both see the images, but by the time he'd reached the end, Ashlee hadn't recognized a single face. The men who had attacked her, including the man at the hospital and hotel, hadn't been among the photos Cecile had pulled.

"What do you think that means?" she asked Lawson.

He shrugged. "Only that they haven't been booked by this department. I'll ask her to expand the search parameters to include other jurisdictions within a hundred-mile radius."

She nodded. Looking at more pictures wasn't exactly how she wanted to spend her day, but she would do whatever it took to find out who was behind these attacks.

Her mouth went dry and she guzzled down the last of her water. "Is there somewhere I can get some more?"

He took her cup and stood. "I'll get it for you. This courthouse is over a hundred and fifty years old and offices have been added piecemeal through the years. It's like a maze if you don't know your way around. You'll have to go through three doorways just to reach the kitchen. I'd hate for you to make a wrong turn and end up in lockup." She smiled at his lighthearted tone, but she expected there was some truth wrapped up in his joking manner. "You wait here. I'll be right back."

He disappeared through a doorway.

Ashlee leaned back in her seat and pulled

the blanket tighter around her shoulders, already missing Lawson's presence. Something about the handsome deputy made her feel safer whenever he was around—and more exposed without him by her side.

Stop it, she told herself. She had to stop being so reliant on Lawson. After the way she'd treated him, he owed her nothing. And after today's near-death experience, he could decide at any moment that protecting her was too risky—and then he'd vanish from her life the way she had from his.

She thought about her apartment and how it had been ransacked. Whoever was after her was dangerous. She would gladly return the money to them if it meant these threats against her disappearing. But yesterday she'd told the man she didn't have the money…and today she'd been attacked anyway.

Why?

She pressed her hands to her forehead and willed herself to remember. It did no good except to give her a slight headache to go with the rest of her aching body.

Lawson returned with another cup of water and she drank it up.

"Why don't we head back to Silver Star," he suggested. "You look like you could use some rest."

"What about the photos?"

"I'll have Cecile email them to me. We can always look through them back at the ranch."

She was glad to leave. As much as she wanted to help track down these men, she was worn out from the afternoon's events and could use some time to work out the kinks in her aching muscles. "Okay."

Lawson told Cecile about their plans, then led Ashlee outside to his brother's truck. She crawled inside and buckled up and they headed out of town and toward Silver Star Ranch. But as she glanced at the people coming and going through town, she couldn't help wondering… Who was out there that wanted her dead?

Once Ashlee was settled upstairs to rest, Lawson headed outside to the barn. Ranch chores were never done and he needed the physical exercise of work, even if it was only cleaning out the stalls, to help him wrap his mind around the attempts on Ashlee's life. And the fact that the shooters hadn't seemed to be bothered by him being in the line of fire, either. No, these men, whoever they were, were dangerous and Ashlee had managed to do something to get into their crosshairs.

His brother Paul appeared in the doorway

and hung some tack on a hook. "Josh told me what happened today. Are you okay?"

Lawson nodded. "We're both okay. Shook up, but that's about it."

"You need to be more careful, little brother."

"I'm being careful, but it's difficult with Ashlee in danger."

"Yeah, I guess I understand that."

"How are you doing?" Paul wasn't always willing to talk about his recovery process from his injury, but Lawson felt it was important to keep asking, to let his brother know that he cared.

"I'm getting there, but I'm sure ready to be back in the action."

Lawson couldn't possibly understand all that Paul was going through. His injuries had been severe and his healing time was taking longer than he wanted. Ranch work was hard, but Lawson imagined it was nothing compared to the training Paul had endured as a Navy SEAL. He had to have lightning-quick reflexes before he could return to active service, and he just wasn't there yet.

Paul left and Lawson returned to the stalls. He was nearly done when Miles appeared in the doorway, his suit bag hanging over his shoulder. "I'm heading back to Dallas," he said. "My boss wants me for an assignment tomorrow. Are you going to be okay with this thing with Ashlee? Because I can probably stall him if you need me here."

He would have liked to have Miles around for support, but his brother had a life to get back to. "We'll be fine. Besides, I've got Paul and Colby and Josh here to help."

He nodded. "Yes, Colby said he could stick around for a few more days." He turned to leave, then stopped. "This thing with Ashlee... Lawson, be careful. And I'm not just referring to the danger she's in."

He nodded, his brother's intentions coming through loud and clear. They were all worried about him and how close he was getting to Ashlee, how attached he was finding himself to having her here. He had to keep reminding himself that she didn't belong at Silver Star. She didn't want to be here. She'd made that perfectly clear six years ago when she'd walked out—stomping on his heart along the way.

Lawson watched as Miles climbed into his car and drove away, then returned to his chores. He was finishing up with the stalls when he heard the whinny of the horses in the pen outside the barn and a soft voice. Lawson walked out to find Ashlee at the split-rail fence, stroking the nose of one of the horses and talking to them. The sight of her took his breath away. She looked so natural, so at home with the animals and her surroundings. Like she belonged at Silver Star.

Stop it, he warned himself as he walked out to meet her and leaned over the fence. "That's Lady. She's my mom's horse."

Ashlee stroked her nose. "She's beautiful." She motioned to the other horses in the pen. "They're all so beautiful."

He heard sincerity in her voice and his hope meter kicked up a notch. She'd never cared for horses in the past. That should have been his first clue that she hadn't wanted to live the ranch life with him. Horses and ranches kind of went hand-in-hand.

He took a chance. "Maybe you'd like to go riding later. We have a mare that's real gentle, perfect for beginners."

She chuckled at his use of that word. "Am I a beginner? I don't even know."

"Well, I can't say how much horse riding you've done lately, but you were always a fair rider. Never cared much for it, though."

"That makes me sad and I don't even know why. I can't put my finger on anything specific, but something about being out here, stroking this horse and taking in the fresh air, makes me feel like I've been inside a box for a really long time and now I've finally been freed from it. It's almost as if the idea of fresh air and green fields is foreign to me."

"I'd imagine you've been working inside for a long while. I get that. This is a far cry from being stuck in some office year after year."

"I guess it is."

He hopped off the fence. "Why don't I saddle up the horses and take you on a tour of the ranch? There's a real pretty spot down by the lake."

She smiled at him, a smile that sent his hopes shooting through the roof.

Calm down, boy.

Her eyes sparkled at the idea. "I'd like that."

He hurried into the barn to retrieve the saddles, but his phone buzzed before he could get to them. He glanced at the text message from Josh.

Bring Ashlee to the office. Someone showed up here looking for her. Says he's her boyfriend.

The boyfriend. Of course, he would show up now. Lawson gave a beleaguered sigh as he slid the phone into his pocket and walked out to the horse pen. "Change of plans. We need to head back to the sheriff's office."

Ashlee's eyes widened with surprise. "What is it? Did they find those men?"

"No, nothing like that. Someone arrived at the station looking for you. He says he's your boyfriend."

"Oh, I forgot about him."

"I thought you forgot about everyone." The bite in his tone was uncalled for, but he'd once again been stung by her and he didn't like that feeling one bit.

"It's not like that. I don't remember him— didn't even recognize his picture when I looked it up online back at the hotel. When I talked to him and told him what was going on, he insisted on coming out here—but then, a few minutes later, I was attacked by that man. I haven't really had much time to think about Jake since then. That's all I meant."

Lawson remembered her saying something about the guy back at the hotel, when she was giving her statement—but he hadn't wanted to think about it, so he'd pushed it from his mind. But now he couldn't ignore him anymore. The one good thing about Ashlee running away was that he hadn't had a front-row seat to her moving on from him. He hadn't had to see her with another man. Not until now.

They climbed into Josh's pickup and Lawson drove her to the sheriff's office, but he was already dreading this reunion for his own sake. He didn't want to see the kind of man Ashlee had left him for. The previous day, she said he was her boss, which meant he was probably wealthy. He knew she worked for a large and successful accounting firm.

They arrived and walked in to find Cecile talking to a man in a suit. He was tall and looked like he'd just stepped out of a cowboy magazine ad. Not a real cowboy, but an ad agency's airbrushed idea of one. Lawson instantly didn't like him and didn't trust him.

He glanced at Ashlee, who was studying the man, too, but he didn't see any flashes of recognition. Not yet.

Cecile motioned behind him and the man turned. A broad smile spread across his face. He rushed over, pulled Ashlee into his arms and hugged her tightly. Too tightly in Lawson's opinion.

"Ashlee, I've been so worried about you," he said, cupping her face in his hands. "How are you? Any recollections returned?"

She continued to stare up at him, but her face was a blank. "No, nothing yet."

Understanding dawned on the man's face

and he took a step back. "You have no idea who I am then, do you?"

"I'm sorry. I don't. I mean, I recognize your voice from our phone conversation and your picture from the web site, but I don't know you."

"That's disappointing. I was hoping just seeing me would spark something."

Lawson understood that disappointment and could empathize with this guy on that point. He, too, had been hurt that she hadn't known him the first time she'd seen him. Of course, in that moment, he hadn't known about the amnesia. He'd thought she'd just forgotten him.

Ashlee turned to him. "This is Lawson Avery. He's an old friend. He's been letting me stay with him and his family during this ordeal."

The man held out his hand to Lawson. "Jake Stephens. Nice to meet you. And thank you for taking such good care of our girl."

Shaking this guy's hand made his skin crawl, but he forced himself to do it and nod. Something about Jake's slick manner Lawson didn't like, but he couldn't be sure it wasn't pure jealousy on his part. He didn't like Jake Stephens one little bit.

Jake slipped his arm around Ashlee and

pulled her to him. "I had to rent a car to drive from the airport, but if we leave now, we may be able to catch a flight back home tonight."

"You can't leave!" Lawson exclaimed and both Jake and Ashlee looked at him. "I mean we—the sheriff's office—still has questions."

Thankfully, Cecile came to his defense and put him out of his jealous misery—although he didn't miss the smirk on her face as she did.

"That's true," she said, stepping into the conversation. "Ashlee was found with a large amount of cash and bullet holes in her car. She'd obviously been involved in a gunfight. In addition, she's been the victim of multiple attempts on her life in the past two days. We need to find out who is behind these attacks and what exactly is going on before she leaves town and our leads dry up."

"Yes," Ashlee agreed. "I can't leave until I know who is after me and why. I could be a sitting duck if I go home without those answers."

Jake Stephens wasn't convinced. "But aren't you a target staying here, too? I can provide security for you at my condo. It'll be much safer than that little apartment you live in."

"We have questions for you, as well, Mr. Stephens," Cecile added.

He stiffened, bristling at her comment. "Questions for me? About what? I don't know anything."

"Still—" Cecile opened the door to the interview room "—if you don't mind answering a few questions, it would help in our investigation."

He glanced at Ashlee, then sighed and gave a half-hearted smile. "Sure, whatever you need."

Cecile followed him into the interview room and closed the door as Ashlee moved closer to Lawson.

"What kind of questions is she going to ask him?"

"You called him from the hotel, right? Is it just a coincidence that you were attacked not long after?"

"I wondered that myself right after it happened." She folded her arms over her chest and hugged herself, worry lining her face. Lawson wanted nothing more than to take her into his arms and tell her everything would be okay, but he didn't. It wasn't his place to do so any longer. It was Jake Stephens's.

And if there was any talk of Ashlee returning home with that guy, Lawson was going to know more about him first.

"Wait here. I'll be right back." He turned to Kyle, whose desk was behind his. "Will you keep an eye on her? I want to hear this."

Kyle nodded and Lawson opened the door to the interview room.

Cecile gave him a look, but continued her questioning. "I understand Ashlee works at your company. Tell me what you do, Mr. Stephens?"

"I'm a partner in an accounting firm. What does that have to do with anything?"

"Ashlee has been the victim of multiple attempts on her life," Cecile replied smoothly. "We're trying to determine where those threats are coming from. Is it possible this is linked to something with her work or your firm?"

The man glanced at them both, then laughed and shook his head. "Trust me, it's boring work most of the time."

"I'm sure that's true, but we would still like to investigate that angle. Are you familiar with a motorcycle gang called the Pontiac Posse? Are they clients of your firm?"

"I've never heard of them before."

Neither had Lawson, but he assumed that

was the biker gang Mayor Baxter had warned them about.

"I'd like your permission to take a look at Ashlee's client list."

"That's not possible, Deputy Bradley. Our clients have a right to privacy."

"But aren't they Ashlee's clients? I'm sure you wouldn't balk at her looking through them."

Jake tapped his finger against the table, then shook his head. "I'm afraid, given the circumstances, I can't allow that. If she's incapacitated, and she obviously is, I'll have to reassign her workload until she's able to continue."

Cecile leaned back in her chair and studied the man. "How long have you and Ashlee been dating, Mr. Stephens?"

"Four months."

"And you care about her?"

"I do, but—"

"Then why are you hampering our ability to discover who is after her?"

"I'm not trying to hamper anything, but I have a responsibility to my company, as well. I can't just hand over confidential files because my girlfriend is in trouble."

Lawson grimaced at the word *girlfriend*,

but tried not to let it show as the man continued.

"Look, I'll go through those files myself and let you know if something jumps out at me."

"No offense, Mr. Stephens, but you're not an investigator. Besides, how can we be certain Ashlee's not in danger because of something that ties back to *you*?"

"I would never hurt Ashlee."

"Then it's a coincidence that an hour after she called you, she was attacked at the hotel?"

His face paled and he leaned back in his seat. "I had nothing to do with that."

"I hope not." Cecile stood and walked from the room. Lawson followed her.

"What do you think?" he asked as they entered the hallway.

Josh appeared from his office and asked the same question. "What's your gut tell you about Stephens?"

Cecile glanced at Josh, then gave a weary sigh. "I don't think he's involved, but I can't rule it out until I see those files."

"And without a warrant, that's not going to happen," Lawson added.

Josh shook his head. "We've got nothing to justify a warrant at this point. Let's run a background check on Stephens and the firm. See if there's any dirt to be found that could get us a look at those files. Actually, call Colby. His connections at the Bureau might reveal something more than ours would. Maybe there's a corruption investigation Mr. Stephens 'forgot' to tell us about."

Cecile nodded. "I'm on it." She walked off to make the call.

Lawson stared at the man through the window as he sat in the interview room, engrossed in texting on his phone. It made sense that whatever Ashlee was involved in had something to do with her job. Her whole life was about her career. It had to be, since she'd left him for it. And if this case was tied to her work, then Jake Stephens was the man who would know about it. Lawson hadn't gotten a dishonest vibe from him, but a good liar could fool even someone trained to spot them.

"If he's involved and he gets back to his office, those files will be gone before we can look at them."

Josh shook his head and motioned to Stephens, who was still texting. "Trust me, brother. If he's involved, they're already gone. But do you really think he is?"

The truth was…no, he didn't. Lawson wanted something sinister from this guy, but his gut told him he was on the straight and narrow and really seemed to care about Ashlee. That burned him, too, because Jake Stephens appeared to be everything he wasn't—successful, ambitious and, most of all, in a relationship with Ashlee.

He walked into the main office and found Ashlee at his desk, using his computer. She flushed as if embarrassed. "I hope you don't mind. Deputy Deaver signed me on. I wanted to check my social media page."

He sat and rolled his chair closer to hers. The worried crease of her forehead told him her sister hadn't left her a message on her page. "Still no word from Bree?"

"No, and I'm worried. Why hasn't she responded to me? Even if she couldn't reach me anywhere else, she could have at least left a post on my page. I would have seen it."

"We've checked her cell phone and bank records. There have been no calls made, no texts, and no movement on her accounts."

"I'm worried about her, Lawson. I have to find her. If this happened to me, she might be in trouble, too."

"Or she might be the cause of this trouble. Have you considered that?"

He saw her eyes flash with something like anger or irritation and knew it was directed at him. He'd seen that look before. For her, it had never mattered that Bree was the author of her own troubles. Ashlee would always run to her aid.

"I'm still trying to run down known associates of your sister. Maybe one of them can lead us to her."

She nodded. "Thank you, Lawson. I know this isn't important to you, but I appreciate your help."

He leaned forward and placed his hand over hers, ignoring the way his heart skipped a beat at the feel of her soft skin and delicate hand under his. "It's important to you, Ashlee, so it's important to me. I'm sorry. I shouldn't be bad-mouthing her to you right now. You're right. Whether or not she's linked to whatever is going on, we need to find her. Finding her might be the only way we learn the answers to why this is happening to you, why someone is targeting you." Lawson nodded at the interview room. "What about Jake? What are you going to tell him?"

"I don't know. I'm certainly not leaving with him. And not just because I need to be here for the investigation. He's a stranger to me. There's nothing familiar about him at all. Plus, I can't get it out of my head that I spoke to him not long before that man showed up at my hotel to attack me. That can't be a co-incidence, can it?"

It could be but, in his experience with criminal cases, coincidences didn't exist.

Josh called both Lawson and Ashlee along with Cecile into his office for a rundown of the investigation.

"We're still trying to track where the money came from," Cecile said. "It's slow going. I'm still waiting on a callback about whether or not it's counterfeit."

"What about that biker gang the mayor mentioned?" Ashlee asked her.

"So far, we haven't been able to tie them to this. We haven't identified any of the men who've attacked you, but if they're a part of that biker gang, they're keeping their heads low. I also checked the call logs and we didn't have any calls about shots fired coming in the day you were found."

"It's unlikely we would, unless they came from town," Josh commented. "Around Courtland County, no one flinches if they hear gunfire."

Cecile interjected. "They would have if they'd heard enough to make all the bullet holes in the back of Ashlee's car. I'd guess those holes were made with a semiautomatic. Either that or there were multiple shooters."

"She's right," Lawson concurred. "That much gunfire would attract attention."

"Which means," Josh noted, "that wherever this happened, it was isolated enough that no one was around to hear the shots. That could mean an abandoned ranch or warehouse."

Lawson took off his hat and rubbed his head. "There are any number of abandoned ranches around here to choose from—too much land to check everywhere."

Cecile stepped forward and glanced at the map of Courtland County pinned to Josh's wall. "That's true, but based on the road and the direction she was headed when you found her, Lawson, I might be able to narrow down that list."

Josh nodded. "Good. Start working on that. And pull Mahoney and Deaver off their assignments if you need the help."

Cecile turned to walk out, but stopped when the front door opened and Colby walked in and headed straight for Josh's office. "Looks like your brother has news."

Lawson stood as Colby entered. "Did you find something?"

"I had a colleague at the Bureau do a check on our friend Jake Stephens in there," Colby said, motioning toward the interview room. "His background came back clean. He's got no criminal record, pays his bills on time and manages a multimillion-dollar company that hasn't been tied to any scandals. The background check revealed no red flags. He emailed me a copy and I printed it out for you."

Lawson took the report from him. Disappointment settled in and he saw by her expression that Ashlee was disappointed, too. They were both getting weary of dead ends. He'd been hoping for something to be wrong with this guy, but that had obviously just been the jealousy talking. He glanced through the printed pages and realized his brother was right. This guy didn't even have a parking ticket in his past. "That doesn't necessarily mean he's not involved. He could have something going on under the table that he hasn't been caught at yet. Ashlee could have found out, which put a target on her back."

"That's always a possibility," Colby said, "but until she remembers what's going on, we're searching for something and we don't even know what it is. I called in a favor and had an agent go down to that firm's headquarters and start asking questions. If there is something going on, she may be able to flush it out, but it's a long shot."

"Sometimes they pay off," Lawson reminded him.

Colby nodded and shoved his hands into his pockets. "Sometimes they do."

"Until then," Josh interrupted, "we've got no reason to hold Stephens. Let's turn him loose."

Lawson glanced at Ashlee. They needed more than a long shot. They needed answers if he was going to keep her safe. But at least she wasn't leaving with Jake Stephens.

FIVE

Jake emerged from the interview room. He'd removed his suit coat and tie and was carrying them slung over his arm as he approached her. "They're letting me go. I guess they believe me that I didn't have anything to do with this."

"They're only doing their jobs." The need to defend Lawson and Cecile and Josh was strong. They'd taken her in and helped her. "They're being careful." And she was thankful for that. She didn't know anything about this man or what he was into.

He gave her a questioning stare. "What about you? Do you believe me?"

She glanced up into his dark eyes, praying for something familiar, some twinge of recognition to hit her, but nothing happened. This man was more of a stranger to her than Lawson. There was no familiarity here, no sense of safety. Just...nothing. It was obvious he wanted something from her, but she couldn't give it. "I'm sorry. I don't know you. I don't remember you."

"I guess that means you really aren't coming home with me then?"

She shook her head. "I need to remain here to figure out what's going on."

Jake rubbed his face, his frustration over this whole encounter showing. "I don't suppose my staying would do any good."

"I don't see how." Ashlee wasn't sure she wanted him to stay. She didn't trust him and it had nothing to do with anything he'd said or done, or any sense of danger she felt. She didn't trust anyone but Lawson. Everyone else in her life was suspect. "Until I figure out what happened to me or get my memories back, I don't know if I can trust you."

"I'm sorry you feel this way. I care about you very much, Ashlee."

She didn't want to hear about his feelings for her. They weren't what was important. She needed answers. "What do you know about my sister, Bree?"

"Not much. I know she recently moved in with you, but I've never met her. I always sensed you and she were close."

How intimately could she have known this man if Ashlee hadn't even shared information about her sister with him? According to Lawson, they'd always had a close relationship, with Ashlee even rushing to bail out Bree when she needed it.

Jake reached out and pushed a strand of hair behind her ear. It was an intimate gesture that she didn't like. It didn't feel right to her, but he seemed oblivious to her discomfort. That seemed like a bad sign.

"Okay. I'll go. But I won't stop worrying about you, Ashlee." He pulled a card from his wallet and handed it to her. "Here's my number in case you misplaced it. I hope you'll remember it soon, but in case you don't and you need anything—anything—phone me and I'll be here."

"Thank you, Jake. I appreciate that." She slipped the card into her jeans' pocket and stared up at him.

He bent to kiss her, but she leaned away from him. She wasn't ready for that.

He took the hint and nodded. "Sorry. Habit."

She couldn't imagine his arms around her or letting him kiss her. Those thoughts only felt right when they involved the cowboy across the room, wringing his hat in his hand, a sliver of jealousy in his blue eyes. She didn't know if she was remembering their past together or just daydreaming, but Lawson was the one who came to her mind when she imagined such things. Maybe she'd never gotten over him, after all, and this was their second chance. She didn't know, but she did know the man standing before her was not the man she wanted to be with. Not now.

But as she walked him outside, he seemed unwilling to leave her. "I'll keep in touch."

"Goodbye, Jake."

"And don't worry about your job, either. It'll be there for you when you're ready to return."

Her job? She hadn't even given that a single thought since this all began, except for looking up herself on the company's web site. She couldn't imagine walking into that office and having no idea what it was she even did there. But she might have to face that exact situation sometime in the future if her memory didn't return.

No, don't think like that. She was going to get her memories back. She had to think positive. It was going to happen.

She watched Jake climb into his rental car and drive away before returning to the safety of Lawson and the ranch. Returning to a life she couldn't remember with a man she didn't know wasn't her first choice, but she also didn't want to be a burden to Lawson and his family. After all, she'd already hurt them so much.

But her mind was still on her sister.

The fact that Bree wasn't responding to Ashlee's messages bothered her. Was she in trouble? Or hurt? Maybe even dead? Could Bree's death be the traumatic event Ashlee had witnessed that had been so horrible she'd blocked all her memories out? She didn't like to even think about that, but she had to consider it. What else could be so terrible that she would want to forget everything?

God, wherever Bree is, please keep her safe and bring her back to me.

With no further information about who was after Ashlee or why, Lawson drove her back to the ranch, grateful she hadn't decided to leave with Jake Stephens, after all. She was safer here than anywhere else and that was important to him.

And his heart wasn't the littlest bit inflated that she'd chosen him over Mr. Money Suit.

His phone rang as they drove and he glanced at it in its cradle on the dashboard. He didn't recognize the number, but it had a Dallas area code. He answered it, curious as to who would be calling him.

"Hello? Deputy Avery, this is Jan McAlpin. We met at the apartment when you and Ashlee came by earlier."

Ashlee was looking at him with curiosity.

"I remember you, Mrs. McAlpin. What can I do for you?"

Ashlee leaned closer to him, excitement already plastered on her face, clearly hopeful for good news. He put the phone on speaker mode so they could both hear.

"I saw Bree at the apartment just a little while ago. She seemed to be fine. I asked her if she'd spoken to Ashlee and she claimed she hadn't seen any messages from her."

"You actually spoke to her?"

"Yes, I did. She's there now, in fact."

"We're three hours away. If you see her trying to leave, stop her. Tell her we're on our way and that her sister needs to speak with her badly." She agreed and he ended the call.

Ashlee's eyes were glowing with happiness. "I'm so relieved to find out she's okay. I've been eating myself up with worry."

He turned the truck around, heading back toward the highway. He phoned Josh to give his brother the update.

"That's good news. Just be careful. Remember what happened the last time you two drove into Dallas."

"Don't worry," Lawson assured him. "I'm keeping watch." Although he didn't mention it to Ashlee, he was concerned their attackers may be watching the apartment, too. Would they see Bree there and try to confront her? Or was she in cahoots with whoever had attacked Ashlee?

He didn't want to believe Bree was connected, but the fact that she'd walked right back into the apartment without fear told him she was either involved or knew nothing about what was going on. If it was the latter, then where had she been for the past few days? Either way, he needed some answers from her.

He drove as fast as he could without breaking the speed limit. He could sense Ashlee was anxious to reach her apartment and get some answers from her sister. Her concern and worry for her sister was, sadly, all too familiar. Bree had spent most of her life giving her sister needless concerns for her safety.

He pulled into the parking lot of the apartment complex and parked the truck. Ashlee hopped out and he hurried to catch up to her as she bolted for the stairs.

She hurried down the breezeway, but something grabbed Lawson's attention before they reached the apartment. The door to her neighbor's unit stood open and Ashlee's cat slipped out and took off. Maybe Mrs. McAlpin had left it open because she was looking for them or listening for Bree to try to leave, but something about it made the hairs on his neck stand on end.

He grabbed Ashlee's arm as she walked in front of the window to the elder woman's apartment and pulled her backward just as bullets went flying through the window. She screamed and he shoved her through Mrs. McAlpin's doorway, slamming the door and locking it as more bullets flew.

Ashlee screamed again and he turned around to see Mrs. McAlpin bound to a chair. She was slumped over, a fatal gunshot wound through her head.

Lawson took out his phone and shoved it at Ashlee. "Call 9-1-1." He pulled his gun from his holster and stood to the side of the front window, trying to get a look at the outside exterior walkway. He didn't have a good line of sight to Ashlee's door, but he saw it open and a hulking figure exited the apartment and headed their way, the shape of a gun in his hands.

Lawson's heart was pounding in his ears, but he remained still, watching and waiting to see if the man approached Mrs. McAlpin's door. Ashlee huddled in the corner, still on the phone with emergency services, as the man stopped in front of the door and the knob turned. Lawson moved back from the door and raised his weapon, his pulse racing at the thought of having to use it. He'd only fired it once during his time with the sheriff's office, but he would shoot if he had to. If it meant getting between this man and Ashlee, he would do it in a heartbeat.

The knob turned again, then again as his attempts to get inside grew more furious. Lawson heard him grunt in frustration. Lawson released the safety on his gun, already sensing what was about to happen. This guy wasn't going to just leave. He'd come too far. He'd killed Mrs. McAlpin to get Ashlee back here and he needed to finish the job by killing Ashlee.

Well, he wasn't going to get to her, not if Lawson had anything to do with it.

The door burst open as it was kicked in. Pieces of wood went flying. Ashlee screamed, but Lawson stood firm, first warning the man to stop, then firing as the man came into view, his weapon raised. Lawson's first bullet hit the man's arm and he jerked backward, but he came back, raising the gun again. Lawson fired a second time and the man hit the ground.

Sirens sounded in the distance. Hearing them, the man scrambled to his feet before Lawson could fire another shot. He took off running down the stairs, then into the woods behind the parking lot.

Only when he was certain the intruder was gone did Lawson turn to check on Ashlee. "Are you okay? Are you hurt?"

She looked up at him with fear shining in her green eyes. "I'm okay."

He pulled her into his arms and she burrowed her head into his shoulder, sobs racking her body.

"Do you think she was here?" Ashlee asked, her breath catching as she sobbed. "Do you think Bree was really here?"

He would need to double-check her apartment, but his gut was telling him no. "Mrs. McAlpin was probably forced to make that call at gunpoint, then once it was done, he shot her."

She glanced over at her neighbor, then pushed her face back into his chest. He pulled his arms around her and held her as her body shook with shock, horror and fear. They'd nearly walked into a trap that had been set to get Ashlee back to her apartment.

He couldn't be that careless again.

Because whoever was after Ashlee would stop at nothing to get to her.

Ashlee was quiet on the drive back to Silver Star. She'd stopped crying, but sadness still hung over her. As he'd expected, there was no sign that Bree had ever returned to her apartment. Mrs. McAlpin had been used as a decoy to lure them there.

He'd phoned Josh to let him know what had happened and, after several hours of recounting the events to the Dallas PD, then searching for Ashlee's cat who'd gone missing in all the commotion, they'd returned home as night fell. They hadn't found the cat, but Lawson had left his number with several neighbors who'd agreed to keep their eyes open for him. He parked, then led her into the house and up to her bedroom, hoping she would get a good night's sleep and feel better tomorrow.

But despite his hopes, he knew the truth. Ashlee wouldn't feel better until she knew what had happened to her sister and who wanted her dead.

When she missed breakfast the next morning, his concern kicked up a notch.

"Give her some time," his dad advised him. "She's been through a lot. She'll work it out on her own and come down when she's ready."

His mother agreed. "I'll take her up a plate. That'll probably make her feel better."

"I'll do it," he offered, but she shooed him away.

"You, go work. There are things to be done."

Lawson slipped on his hat and walked outside, knowing his parents were right. She needed time and space right now and he would give that to her. But, as he headed for the barn, he spotted her at Kellyanne's window staring down at him. He took off his hat and gave her a little wave, happy to see that she returned it.

He went about his chores and after a while spotted Paul and their part-time ranch hand, Zeke, saddling up two horses in the barn.

"What's going on?" he asked his brother.

"We're going out to check the fence line to see if any repairs are needed. I want to show Zeke what to look for and how to make repairs. Figured we'd take the horses out instead of the ATVs."

"I know what a broken fence looks like and how to repair it," Zeke stated. Lawson didn't doubt him. The kid was only twenty-two, but he'd been around ranches all of his life, having grown up on his uncle's ranch on the other side of town. He'd taken the job at Silver Star to supplement his income while he attended the local community college.

Zeke probably didn't need a lesson, but it wouldn't hurt him to learn how they did things at Silver Star. Plus, Lawson knew Paul was restless—and he wasn't wrong to think the fences needed checking. With only Lawson on the ranch, the outlying fences and borders had likely been breached by kids out riding or hunters.

"That's a good idea. I'll saddle up and help."

Paul nodded. "We'll start at the east fence line. You start at the west." With that decided, Paul and Zeke mounted their horses and took off.

Lawson went back to the house to check on Ashlee before he headed out and was thrilled to find her with his mother shelling peas.

He leaned against the doorway and noticed she looked better today.

"Everything okay?" she asked when she spotted him.

"Everything's great," he told her, unable to stop the smile he was sure was spreading across his face at how nice she looked sitting there, helping his mother. She looked more at ease in this house now than she ever had been with her memory intact—and back then, she'd never before been one to jump in and offer to help. Another clue he'd missed that she hadn't been cut out for ranch life where surviving depended on everyone pulling their weight. "I need to go check out some fence lines. Are you going to be okay here?"

"I'd love to go with you." Her face was full of excitement as she turned to him, and he thought the fresh air and sunshine was just what she needed.

"We did talk about taking a ride, didn't we?"

Excitement bubbled in her eyes, but then she glanced at his mother and what she was doing. Before she could protest, Diane took charge. "You go ahead. I'll manage this."

Ashlee slipped on a pair of his sister's cowboy boots and his heart skipped a beat when she stared up at him from beneath the hat he'd grabbed to keep the afternoon sun from bearing down on her. She looked like a right fine cowgirl and it got his mind racing again with foolish thoughts that this was the place where she belonged.

He saddled up the gentlest of their mares for her to ride since he had no idea how long it had been since she'd been in the saddle— not to mention her lack of riding memories.

Once upon a time, he'd been planning to give her a horse as a wedding gift. He'd sold the mare after Ashlee ran away. He couldn't bear to look at the horse any longer and wanted a home for her where she would mean something good to someone. But today, seeing the way Ashlee's hair curled at her neck beneath the cowboy hat and the way she managed the mare, she looked so authentically at home that it took his breath away.

He slipped onto his horse and they headed out. She wasn't as steady on the mare as he remembered her being, but he could chalk that up to her amnesia and lack of recent practice. She soon found her stride and had the mare in a gentle gallop. The smile that stretched across her face warmed his heart and he pushed his horse to keep up with her. He wanted to tell her to take it slow, but he enjoyed seeing her appreciate the horse and the experience.

They rode along the fence line and he spotted a gap. He hadn't thought to bring any tools to fix it, so he made a note of the location, then headed for the lake. He didn't want to push Ashlee too far on her first outing even if she did seem to be enjoying the ride.

She pulled the horse to a stop as she soaked in the landscape. "It's beautiful country here. Even the air smells cleaner. This place is beautiful, Lawson. Thank you for bringing me."

He did his best not to get his hopes up at her words, but she wasn't making it easy for him. Her presence was at once a painful reminder of his broken heart and a flicker of hope at what could be. She'd never been this appreciative of the place before. Was it just the amnesia or had her attitude truly changed? "I'm glad to hear it. Has it sparked anything?"

"No, but it is familiar. This place...it feels like home." She turned and smiled at him and his heart soared. He'd never heard Ashlee refer to this place as home even when it nearly was.

"Why don't we let the horses take a rest?" He slid off his horse, then helped her down, grabbing her waist and holding her against him longer than he needed to. She didn't resist. All his senses went on high alert at being so near to her again and a dizzying current of electricity sparkled between them. His pulse quickened as she leaned into him, lifting her face to his eagerly. He cupped her face in his hands as his lips claimed hers. They were soft and sweet and willing.

He wasn't being smart in getting his hopes up, but it had been six long years that they'd been apart. Yet he'd never stopped thinking of her, hoping that she might one day realize how much she missed this place...and him.

But then the image of Jake Stephens crowded into his thoughts. She hadn't spent those years waiting for him. This wasn't his Ashlee and she could never be, amnesia or no, because his version of Ashlee was a figment of his imagination, an idealized version that didn't exist.

That thought grabbed hold of him and he released her, putting several steps between them as he struggled to regain his composure. He knelt and picked at the grass, tossing blades of it into the wind. It was a nervous habit, but he needed something to do with his hands when every instinct was telling him to pull her into his arms, kiss her again and worry about the future in the future.

Ashlee sat beside him, curling her legs beneath her. She seemed so carefree in spite of all she'd been through, and what had just happened between them.

"I'm sorry. That shouldn't have happened," he said, struggling to clear his throat enough to speak normally.

"I didn't mind." She stared at him, her eyes sparkling.

"You have a boyfriend," he reminded her.

"Oh, right. I keep forgetting him." The smile on her lips told him she was making light of her amnesia. It was both amusing and endearing. Also, completely frustrating.

She glanced out at the lake throwing reflective light off the water and took in a deep breath. "Were you serious before when you said I didn't care for this place?"

He nodded. "You always felt it was too slow paced for your tastes. You wanted something faster with more action."

She shook her head. "I certainly don't feel that now. It's lovely here. I can't imagine wanting to be anywhere else."

His heart leaped at her words, but he had to keep calm. She didn't know what she was saying. Maybe she felt this way now, but that would surely change when her memories returned and she recalled how much she loved the hustle and bustle of city life. He couldn't risk falling for her again because of an impulsive kiss and a comment made while caught up in the moment. He wouldn't be able to survive another heartbreak like the last time.

He had to guard his heart from her.

He stood and walked to the bank of the lake and she followed, slipping her hand into his so easily that if a shiver hadn't run down his spine, he might not have even noticed. But it had and he did. He had to keep his wits about him. He'd told her about her leaving, but he hadn't shared how devastated and shattered it had left him. If it hadn't been for Silver Star and the solace it gave him, he wasn't sure he would have made it through those dark days.

"I can't afford to fall for you again, Ashlee. What happens when you get your memory back and remember that you don't love me?"

"Who says that's going to happen? Maybe I'll remember how much I want to be here— how much I regret leaving."

He wanted that to be true and opened his mouth to tell her so when a shot rang out and he jerked as something stung his gut and pain rushed through him. His knees buckled and he fell, hitting his head on a rock and sliding into the lake. His vision blurred, but he heard Ashlee scream and the horses whinny and bolt as another shot rang out. Water surrounded him and darkness flowed over him, and all he could think was that he had to help Ashlee.

But there was nothing he could do to help her as he lost consciousness.

Ashlee jumped behind a cluster of rocks as Lawson splashed into the water. She took cover and scanned the area. She couldn't see who or where the shots came from, but she heard two more, one of them hitting a tree behind her, causing her to scream again.

Lawson was still in the lake, his legs on

the bank and his head in the water. He wasn't moving. Unless she could get to him to pull him out, he would drown before he regained consciousness. But if she left the shelter of these rocks, the shooter would surely fire again.

She didn't know what to do. Lawson's face was nearly submerged and he still hadn't moved. His time was running out. She had to make a decision. Hide or risk it to save his life?

She decided to risk it. She couldn't let him drown.

She crept out from behind the rocks. Another shot rang out, hitting the stone and breaking off a chunk that splattered in front of her, spraying rocks into her face. She shrieked and retreated behind the formation. She was pinned down and although she couldn't see the shooter, she suspected he was perched in the tree line a few hundred yards away. She was trapped and Lawson's time was running out.

She cried out to God for help and something returned to her. Not a memory, but a feeling so strong and raw that she knew it had to be real. Dread and shame rushed through her that she'd caused this to happen to Lawson.

But Lawson shouldn't have to pay for her mistakes.

She hadn't meant to put his life at risk, but it had happened, and she would never forgive herself if he died because of it. She should never have come here, no matter the danger against her, but she hadn't been able to resist the pull of this place and the safety it represented.

Well, it wasn't so safe now.

She glanced at Lawson again and saw the water turning red around him. He was bleeding. She had to get to him. Yet even if she could reach him, how would they get past the shooter to find help?

Suddenly, the sound of galloping hoofs approached and she very nearly collapsed with relief when she spotted Paul and another rider headed her way on horseback. Both had their rifles raised. As they neared, Paul started firing toward the tree line and the other man followed suit. Their horses roared past her and Ashlee took the opportunity to hurry to the water.

She waded in and reached for Lawson, who was still unconscious and bleeding from the stomach. She grabbed him by the shirt and tried to pull him out, but he was too heavy for her to budge once they reached the bank. She couldn't free him completely from the lake alone. All she could do was wait for Paul to return to help her.

Ashlee stroked Lawson's face as the afternoon sun bore down on them. She ran her finger over his strong jaw and unshaved stubble. The wound on his head didn't look bad, though it had been enough to knock him out. The injury to his side, however, was bleeding heavily. He needed to get to a doctor. Where was Paul? It seemed like he'd been gone for so long. Hopefully, he'd captured whoever was shooting at them. Surely, he'd run him off at least. But if so, why hadn't he returned?

She stared at Lawson's face, noticing how pale he'd grown. Tears pooled in her eyes as fear pulled through her. He'd been shot trying to protect her. Lawson had taken the bullet meant for her.

Heavy footfalls sounded and she turned to see Paul's friend break through the tree line before reining his horse to a stop and jumping off.

"It's okay. I'm a friend. My name's Zeke," he said as he rushed over to help her with Lawson.

"Did you get him?" she asked.

"Paul is still trying to track him down. He sent me back here to help."

"He was hit when the gunfire started. He fell and hit his head on the rocks."

Zeke grabbed Lawson under the shoulders and pulled him onto the bank with a strength Ashlee couldn't match. He then dropped to his knees and checked Lawson's breathing, his pulse and, finally, his injuries. "Looks like the bullet only grazed him, but it's bleeding pretty badly." He pulled off his top shirt, wadded it up, then grabbed her hand and pressed the shirt on top of the wound. "Hold your hand here and press down to stop the bleeding."

He pulled out his phone from his pocket and made a call. "Lawson's hurt. We need to get him to the hospital. We're by the lake. Paul and I heard gunfire, then saw two men shooting at Lawson and Ashlee. Paul's still out there searching." Zeke ended the call. "Help is on the way."

She glanced at the shirt and noticed blood was already soaking it. Lawson needed help and quick. Given how long it had felt before Zeke returned—even though it had actually only been minutes—she wondered if whoever he had called would arrive in time.

"How did you find us?" she asked.

Zeke knelt beside Lawson and monitored

his breathing. "We heard the shots so we headed this way."

After what seemed like an eternity, she heard a loud noise and looked up to see an ATV followed by a pickup truck approaching. The ATV stopped and Zeke rushed to the driver—Lawson's brother Colby. He spoke to Colby, then motioned in the direction Paul had gone.

"Get him to the hospital. I'll go help Paul," Colby hollered as he took off on the ATV.

The pickup pulled to a stop and Lawson's mother and father got out and hurried over. Diane knelt beside Lawson and pushed Ashlee's hands away to examine the wound, then replaced them. "We have to bandage this up until we get him to the hospital." Marshall handed over a first-aid kit and she pulled out bandages and gauze and dressed the wound.

Ashlee was pulled aside, but Marshall took a blanket from the truck and wrapped it around her shoulders. "Thank you."

A moment later, the brothers returned.

"What did you find?" Marshall asked.

Paul pulled his horse to a stop. "Tire tracks by the back gate. They drove in here in a truck, but they're long gone now."

His father seemed to take that in before turning back to the problem at hand. "Both of you get over here and help us load Lawson into the truck."

Paul slid off the horse and Colby shut off the ATV. Together with Zeke, the men carried Lawson to the truck and loaded him into the backseat. Ashlee crawled in with him while his parents got into the front.

"The horses Lawson and Ashlee were riding took off at the gunfire. Zeke and I will hang back to find them," Paul stated.

Colby pushed his hands through the window and held his mother's hands for a moment. "And I'll make sure everything is secured back at the house. I'll also call Miles and Kellyanne. They'll want to know."

Ashlee couldn't see Lawson's mother's expression from her spot in the backseat, but she noticed the way the older woman's shoulders shook as she released her son's hands. "We'll call with news," she told him as her husband cranked the engine and took off.

Everyone in the truck was silent on the drive. Lawson still hadn't regained consciousness by the time they reached the emergency room. Ashley watched as the hospital personnel loaded Lawson onto a gurney, then disappeared into the building. She couldn't do anything for him and she couldn't even form the words to express her overflowing emotions in prayer.

Once they were inside, she fell to a chair and put her hands over her face as the tears flowed.

He'd looked so dead, so eerily still in the water. Dread filled her as she imagined what she would do without him. Selfish, yes, but she had no one else she trusted to keep her safe.

"Don't you worry," Diane told her, taking the seat beside her. "He'll be fine. He's a fighter. All my children are fighters."

Ashlee was sure that was true. This family had already shown her they weren't afraid to take a risk. She should feel safe surrounded by them, but fear gripped her. She was in trouble, terrible trouble, and she had no idea what she had done to solicit such danger. Where had that money come from and what had she been doing with it? She just didn't know.

Paul and Colby arrived later and Diane spoke to both Miles and Kellyanne on her cell phone as they waited. Finally, the ER doctor appeared and the family stood, surrounding him.

"He's awake and alert. The damage from the bullet wasn't substantial, but he hit his head when he fell. You'll need to watch him for a concussion."

Diane hugged her husband then Ashlee, but she was calm and collected as she turned to the doctor. "He's got a hard head, Doctor. All my boys do."

"I'm sure he does. We want to keep him for observation, but he's determined to return home. Perhaps you could convince him to stay?"

Marshall shook his head. "I doubt we'll be able to do that. When he's determined about something, he usually gets his way. Besides, my wife used to work as a nurse. She'll know what to watch for."

The doctor nodded. "I'm glad to hear he'll have people to look after him. If he displays any slurring of speech or vomiting, I want you to bring him back in."

Ashlee was incredibly relieved he was going to be okay and that he had a good support system. She wished she had something like that. For all she knew, she did have it, yet even as she had the thought, tears pressed against her eyes and she knew it was not true. If she did, then why did she have such a longing in her gut for it? She couldn't get past the horrible certainty that her life was isolated and she was alone. Those feelings of dread and shame she'd felt earlier resurfaced.

Lawson looked pale as a nurse pushed him to the entrance in a wheelchair over Lawson's protests that he was capable of walking. Ashlee doubted he could do so easily and was glad they were making him take it easy. As his brothers surrounded him, she was assured they would make certain he didn't over-exert himself.

"We'll go get the truck and pull it around," his father told them before he and Diane exited the hospital.

Colby, Paul and Josh waited with her and Lawson.

"You guys can go," Lawson told them.

Josh shook his head. "We'll wait to help you into the truck first and then I need to get back to the office."

"And we need to get back to the ranch," Paul stated, motioning to him and Colby. "We still need to find those horses that bolted. Zeke searched after we left, but he sent me a text earlier that he couldn't find them."

"What about the person who shot me? Did you find him?"

The brothers glanced at one another, then Josh shook his head. "Not yet, but we will."

Something about their expressions told

Ashlee that, despite their initial hesitation when she'd first arrived, they were now squarely intent on closing this case, if only so they could find out who had shot their brother. That act alone had pulled the full force of the Avery brothers into the mix, which meant she'd now allowed an entire family to put themselves in harm's way.

Lawson reached for her hand. "I'm okay," he assured her, as if he could see the guilt written across her face.

He was okay for now, but that image of him lying unconscious in the water would forever haunt her. He'd nearly died taking a bullet for her.

She glanced over his shoulder to the coffee bar in the hospital's foyer. His parents would be several minutes walking to the parking garage then getting the truck. "I'm going to grab a cup of coffee and a muffin," she told him. "Can I get you something?"

"No, I'm not hungry. You go ahead."

He must have sensed her need to get out from under the scrutiny of her brothers because he squeezed her hand, then released it quickly. She hurried to the coffee bar and ordered a small cup and two muffins, thinking he might change his mind and want one later.

As the barista turned away to fix her drink,

she sensed someone suddenly beside her and felt a sharp object press against her side and a hand clamp over her mouth.

"Make a sound and I'll gut you," the man sneered.

She glanced toward where Lawson and his brothers were still by the door, talking. Not one of them was looking this way. Even the barista hadn't turned around. No one was watching as the man dragged her away.

SIX

Lawson heard something fall and glanced at the coffee bar to see an overturned chair and the barista calling Ashlee's name, but Ashlee wasn't there.

"Ashlee! She's gone."

His brothers sprang into action, each one running past the coffee bar to search for her while Lawson wheeled himself over and saw Ashlee's wallet had fallen on the floor. He grimaced as he bent over and picked it up.

"Where's the woman this belongs to?" he asked the barista. "Did you see where she went?"

The girl's eyes widened in fear at his frantic tone. "I didn't. One minute she was there, but when I turned around the next, she was gone."

He wheeled himself down the hallway to the elevators. He didn't know where his brothers had gone, but they'd surely spread out to search. He hated being in this chair, but he could move faster in it than he could walk right now.

At the end of the elevator entrance hall was a door with a keypad lock that he thought led to the emergency department. He banged on it, hoping someone would hear and open it, but he stopped when a cry from the stairwell grabbed his attention. He turned around and headed toward it. Whoever'd taken Ashlee must have been hiding there because he heard her cry out again. He pushed to his feet, ignoring the pain that was stabbing at his side, and opened the door. He leaned over the railing to see Ashlee being dragged behind a figure dressed all in black, with a cap shielding his face. They were two stories below Lawson's position and heading for the basement floor.

"Ashlee!" he called.

The man stopped and glanced up before picking up his pace, pulling her along behind him while trying to cover her mouth to keep her from crying out. But as he ran, he struggled to keep hold of her.

"Lawson!" she screamed when his hand slipped. Her captor quickly covered her mouth again and kept going.

Lawson didn't know how he would keep

up with them, but he wasn't going to let her out of his sight again. He used the railing to hurry down the steps as best he could, ignoring the pain digging into him with each step.

"Lawson, run! Get help," she cried, grabbing hold of the railing and slowing the man's descent, but he must have done something to threaten her because she cried out in pain then moved with him.

Lawson stumbled over the railings. If he had to, he would jump on top of the man. He didn't care how much it would hurt or how badly it would aggravate his injury. He wasn't letting Ashlee out of his line of sight.

The man lifted a gun from Ashlee's side and fired up at Lawson. He stumbled backward, away from the railing, and the bullet bounced off the concrete behind him but didn't hit him. It only served to push him on. Ashlee was in danger and he couldn't allow this guy to disappear with her, despite how his body was protesting.

A door at the bottom burst open and Lawson heard Josh's booming voice shout, "Let her go!"

Ashlee managed to slip through her kidnapper's grip as the man turned the gun on Josh. His brother fired without hesitation, but missed as the man shoved past him and out the stairwell door. Ashlee ran up the stairs screaming as Josh scrambled back to his feet and out the door.

Lawson sat on a step as Ashlee ran to him and threw her arms around him. He soaked in her presence, the scent of her hair mixed with adrenaline and fear. She was safe and that was all that mattered now. His own guilt and helplessness to protect her was something he could worry about later. He was just thankful his brother had been there to stop her from being hurt.

Josh returned after several minutes, sweaty and out of breath, and looked up at them. "We got him. He's dead. You both okay?"

Lawson gave him a thumbs-up, but he couldn't speak between the pain of his wounds, the way his heart was hammering with fear, and the gratefulness gushing inside him that she was safe.

Ashlee remained with Lawson even when they took him back to the emergency department to have his wounds rebandaged. He'd torn stitches trying to reach her.

She shuddered at the memory of the man's hands on her and the helplessness she'd felt at not being able to even cry out. She should have stayed close to Lawson, yet she'd allowed her emotions to cloud her better judgment. Whoever it was that was after her had to have been watching her closely to take such a risk to grab her with Lawson and his brothers standing only a few feet away.

That meant they were serious about getting to her.

Yet she still didn't know why. She'd already told them the money was at the sheriff's office. Why did they keep coming after her?

And why had she still not heard from her sister?

She jumped as the door swung open and Josh and Colby entered the room. Josh looked tired and she knew he'd just spent the last hour processing the scene downstairs. He'd shot her abductor and although she hated the loss of life, she was grateful he'd been there.

Lawson sat up and grimaced in pain but seemed to push through. "What's going on?" he asked his brothers.

Josh handed him a file and he opened it on the bed.

Ashlee stood and glanced over his shoulder at a photo of the man who'd grabbed her.

"We ran the guy's prints," Josh said. "His name is Marlon Miller. He has a long and dangerous criminal history. Multiple violent crimes in multiple states across the southeast.

He's been under investigation by the DEA, ATF and DOJ for being a high-ranking member of a multistate drug distribution ring. He was a bad dude and I have no doubt he would have killed you, Ashlee."

She had no doubt about the man's proclivity to violence, either, but it didn't explain why he'd been after her. "But what dealings would I have had with a drug ring?"

Lawson looked grim. "Could be this ties back to your job, after all. Maybe he or someone else in the organization could be a client of Jake Stephens's? You saw or heard something you weren't supposed to?"

Colby shook his head and sat. "My friend at the Bureau hasn't found any indications of wrongdoing tied to Brooke and Stephens, and there are no active investigations into the firm's dealings. If he's involved in something nefarious, he's keeping it quiet."

Lawson turned to look at her, his expression grim. "Then it may have to do with the one person in your life that we know has ties to drug dealers."

Bree. He was talking about Bree. "I know she's had her problems, but I can't believe Bree is connected to a multistate drug operation."

"But you don't know for sure, do you?"

"I know," she insisted. "Call it twin intuition or whatever, but I *know* she wouldn't let anyone hurt me. If anything, she's in trouble. She's a victim."

Lawson wouldn't relent. "She was into drugs when I knew her."

"Six years ago," Ashlee fired back. He had no clue what her life since then had been like. None of them did.

"And years of our lives before that. She was bad news, Ashlee. It's possible she's gotten you into something terrible."

"No, she was trying to clean up her life."

"So maybe whoever she was involved with didn't want to let her go," Josh suggested.

Lawson nodded his head. "She was always dragging you down into her messes. That has to be what happened here."

Ashlee folded her arms across her chest and tried to keep her emotions in check. She didn't like the direction the conversation had taken. "That doesn't explain where the money came from or why I had it."

Josh ended their debate. "I say we run Bree's history and try to find out if any known associates are connected to this cartel. That should settle this once and for all."

She finally agreed, just because Lawson was so certain, but also because it would give her more information about her sister. Her gut was telling her Bree wasn't involved—not willingly, anyway—and that she was sincere about trying to get her life together. But was that just wishful thinking? Was Lawson right about Bree being such a screwup? Had she knowingly gotten Ashlee into a dangerous situation?

Ashlee's gut told her no, but the truth was that no one except Bree knew for certain, and the fact that she still hadn't contacted Ashlee made her worry that Lawson was right. Her sister's past may have placed them both in danger.

The nurse on duty had tried one last time to convince Lawson to stay at the hospital for observation, but his answer again was no. He was glad to be back home, back to the safety of the ranch.

Only, Silver Star wasn't so safe anymore.

He was concerned that someone had breached their property to reach Ashlee. He'd thought she was safe within their boundaries, but that wasn't true. These men would do whatever it took to get to her...and Lawson and his brothers still had no idea why.

Marlon Miller had died trying to abduct her and had taken any answers with him to the grave. They didn't even know for certain if he was the one who'd shot at him and Ashlee by the lake. Being on the wrong side of a drug ring meant an entire organization with multiple bad guys on the hunt.

His mom came in and tried to get him to take a pain pill but Lawson refused. He wanted to keep his wits about him. He'd already failed at protecting Ashlee once because of his injuries. He didn't want to add a drugged-out mental state to that if something else happened.

Ashlee sat on the couch beside him and he covered her hand with his and soaked in the feel of her against him and the gentle scent of her hair as she moved. He was happy to be home with the normal sounds of everyday life: his father's gentle snoring as he fell asleep in his recliner, the hum of crickets outside the window, and his mother's soft voice as she read aloud from her Bible.

It was comforting to hear her speak verses. He'd learned much of what he knew about the Bible from her readings. But he had to admit, he'd pulled away from God after Ashlee had left him. He knew it had hurt his mother, but he'd just been so angry at God for not allowing him to see Ashlee's doubts more clearly. He should have sent a lightning bolt or something to alert Lawson that things hadn't been right.

He glanced at Ashlee as she sat and listened. Even now, he didn't blame her for leaving him. He wasn't angry at her for what she'd done. He'd take all the blame for not being enough for her. Well, him and God had split that blame. It hadn't been right and it hadn't been fair, but now he wasn't sure how to crawl back out from under that distance he'd created from his Heavenly Father. Or how to thank Him for bringing Ashlee back into his life.

Lawson didn't even realize he'd drifted off to sleep until he heard the sound of boots on the front porch.

He jerked awake as the front door opened and Colby and Paul entered. They slipped out of their hats and boots as Lawson sat up, anxious for news about the missing horses his brothers had set out to find.

"They're fine," Paul announced. "Found them both by Riker's field. Muddy and hungry, but okay. We stalled them so they could get some food and water, then I'll go back out and groom them." He touched his stomach and glanced toward the kitchen. "Speaking of food, what's for supper?"

His mother laughed and stood, marking the

spot in her Bible for later use. "In all the excitement, I forgot to cook anything. I've got some left over pork chops in the refrigerator. I'll heat them up with some corn and greens."

"Sounds yummy," Colby said, following along behind his brother. "I'll help you."

Lawson stood despite the pounding in his head and the pain ripping at his hip. "Let's go for a walk," he suggested to Ashlee. He was tired of sitting on the sidelines and, even though he trusted his brothers implicitly, he wanted to see for himself that the horses were okay. He saw his brothers turn around to protest and cut them off before they could. "I'm fine," he assured them. "We won't go far. We'll stay by the barn."

Paul studied him, then nodded. "Don't try to groom those horses, Lawson. I'll take care of it."

He nodded at his brother's instructions and got his meaning. Look but don't touch for tonight. He'd follow the instructions, but he thought the mares might be comforted by seeing him. He certainly would be by making sure they were okay.

He reached out for Ashlee's hand and, after a moment's hesitation, she took it and stood. "Are you sure it's safe?"

"We'll be fine. They wouldn't dare come this close to the house."

He slipped on his hat, glad to see someone had retrieved it for him, and his boots and stepped outside. It was warm, still hot and stuffy from the afternoon's heat, but the sky was lit up with stars.

He draped his arm over her shoulder as they walked to the barn. Lawson checked on the horses, glad to see they were in good shape after their ordeal. The fact that they hadn't returned home said something about how terribly they'd been frightened. He still remembered the look on Ashlee's face when he'd been shot as well as his own feeling of helplessness at being unable to move when she'd needed him most. He would make certain it didn't happen again.

Being out here, Ashlee in his arms under the night sky. This was what he remembered most about their relationship. This and talking about problems with her sister. It was like old times.

He had to keep reminding himself that they didn't want the same things. When all this was over, when Ashlee's memories returned, she would remember that she didn't want to be here and that she didn't want to be with him. If he let himself fall for her again, his heart would shatter.

Ashlee was in danger. That was where his focus needed to be.

On protecting her. And on protecting his heart from her.

Ashlee awoke early to the sound of a car door slamming outside. She crawled off the bed and glanced out the window to see Cecile standing by her truck. She was having a conversation with Josh. They both glanced at the house before walking inside.

She dressed quickly and rushed downstairs, happy to see Lawson up and moving around better than he had been the day before. She was still worried about him and the way he'd placed himself at risk because of her, but for now, she needed to hear whatever Josh and Cecile had to tell her.

The smell of coffee and bacon greeted her as she entered the kitchen. Everyone turned to look at her and she noticed their expressions were grim. Whatever news Cecile had come to deliver, it wasn't good.

Cecile had been checking into Bree's past and known associates, so this terrible news had to be about Ashlee's sister. Had they found her? If they had, their frowns made her fear they hadn't found her alive.

She took a seat at the table and tried her

best to brace herself for whatever was coming. "Tell me." Her voice sounded calmer than she felt as tears threatened to overtake her.

Cecile glanced at Josh, who gave her the go-ahead-and-tell-her nod. "As you know, I've been doing some digging into your sister. I pulled her criminal history and discovered she has several arrests for drug possession dating back ten years." She handed Ashlee a file, which she opened. Bree's mug shot stared back at Ashlee, her face rail-thin and her eyes hollow. She'd obviously been in a dark place when this photo had been taken and sadness swept over Ashlee. But this was ancient history if her neighbor's account was to be believed. She glanced at their faces, not understanding. "Okay, so we already knew about her drug use. According to this, her last arrest was nearly two years ago."

"There's more," Cecile said. "This morning, we received a BOLO referencing your sister. Dallas PD believe she's been kidnapped."

All the air left Ashlee's lungs as fear took hold of her. She'd known deep inside that her sister was in danger—that that was why she hadn't been in touch. "What…h-how…" She stumbled over her words. "How do they know that?"

She handed Ashlee the BOLO printout. "Dallas police discovered the body of Travis Lindale. He died of an apparent overdose four days ago. He's on the list of your sister's known associates. Apparently, he was her boyfriend."

Ashlee stared at the crime scene images and shuddered. She recognized the man from the photographs on her sister's social media page. A wave of sorrow she couldn't explain swept over her. She attributed it to worry over her sister and the fact that someone Bree cared about was dead. "And how does that suggest my sister was kidnapped?"

"During the course of their investigation, the police pulled Travis's phone records and discovered a text message indicating that Travis had stolen from the drug organization he worked for. The text demanded that he return what he took or his girlfriend would die." She handed Ashlee a photocopy of the text. "And there was an image attached."

Ashlee glanced at it and gasped. It was a photo of her sister, beaten and holding a newspaper. Terror shone on her face. Ashlee closed her eyes as everything she'd feared was confirmed. "The date on that newspaper is from four days ago."

She glanced at the image of Travis again. "Did they kill him?"

"The coroner ruled it accidental overdose."

"Why would Dallas PD run the phone records of someone who overdosed?" Lawson asked.

"Because Travis Lindale was under investigation by Dallas PD and the DEA because of his employers."

Ashlee set down the papers before she dropped them. Her hands were shaking so badly, she clasped them together to keep from losing control.

Lawson's mother touched her shoulder. "Ashlee, let me get you some breakfast or some coffee."

She shook her head, the mere thought of food making her stomach roil. The smell of coffee and bacon, so inviting moments before, now made her nauseated.

"Some water, then?" Diane continued.

That she agreed to and took a small sip, then placed the glass on the table. "If Travis stole the money from the drug ring, how did I end up with it?"

Josh folded his arms. "We don't know. It's possible you went looking for your sister, found Travis and the phone—it's still unaccounted for—and took the money, possibly trying to save Bree yourself."

"Until something went wrong," Lawson added.

She stared at him and understood his meaning. Her car had been riddled with bullets and something terrible enough for her to block out her life had occurred. Yes, something must have gone very wrong.

"There's more," Cecile continued. "The text message indicated the ransom drop was right here in town at the old stable on your grandparents' property."

"That explains why you were in town," Lawson said.

It all made sense now about what had happened. Her sister had been abducted and was possibly dead if the ransom drop had gone bad—which it must have for Ashlee to still have the money and the bullet holes in her car.

Cecile stood. "I've put together a team to go check out the stables. Maybe we'll find some clues about what happened there."

Josh set down his coffee cup. "Give me a minute. I'll come with you."

Colby stood. "I'll come, too."

"And me," Paul added.

What if they found Bree there—dead? All because Ashlee hadn't been able to finish the job. Hadn't been able to rescue her sister from kidnappers. She'd known something was wrong. She'd known her sister was in trouble. Why hadn't she done more? "I want to go, too."

"That's not a good idea," Lawson intoned. "It might be dangerous. You should stay here at the ranch."

"So should you," Josh insisted.

Lawson stood. "Not a chance." Yet the beads of sweat on his brow made it painfully clear he was hurting. Still, his jaw was set in determination.

"Lawson, you just got out of the hospital yesterday. You need to take it easy and re-cover," his mother said.

"I'm going and that's final."

Well, he wasn't going alone. "I'm going, too," she persisted. He turned and started to protest but she cut him off. "I'm going. This is my sister and this is my family's property. I won't be left behind."

Finally, Cecile sighed and collected her papers. "Fine, but you two are both remaining in the car until the first team goes inside," she said.

Ashlee was okay with that. She wasn't interested in stepping into any more danger than necessary, and she certainly didn't want Lawson taking risks or pushing himself too hard and getting injured again.

As Cecile and the men gathered their stuff and headed outside, Ashlee felt some excitement that they were finally making progress. Yet that sense of dread had returned, causing her thoughts to turn to her sister and what had happened to her.

She only hoped when they found Bree, they would find her alive.

Lawson checked his gun as they approached the turnoff, driving through the decaying entrance where a lopsided sign dubbed the place Taylor Ranch. The barn was at the back of the land on a dirt road.

Josh was driving. Although he wasn't happy that Lawson was tagging along, he hadn't forbidden it. He must have known better, must have seen in Lawson's face that he was going regardless. If something had happened to Bree that had resulted in Ashlee's being mixed up in something nefarious, Lawson wanted to be there to see it for himself. Because he'd vowed to protect Ashlee from any danger—and that included the danger she might cause herself by trying to help Bree. Above all else, Ashlee loved her sister. She would do anything for her.

There were no cars around as they passed by the old house, which was falling into disrepair. Josh stopped at the barn and they all hopped out. Their weapons were at the ready, even though the fact that no cars surrounding the barn indicated no one was there. If anything, this case had taught them that they couldn't be too careful. Tire marks in the dirt indicated that the path had been disturbed recently. As far as he knew, this property had been abandoned since Ashlee's parents had moved away. Just another abandoned property like many others around the county. There was no reason for anyone to be out here—no good reason, anyway.

Three cars pulled in behind them, carrying Cecile, Paul, Colby and a handful of other deputies. Josh, Cecile and two deputies approached the barn. Cecile coordinated the breach of the barn while Lawson sat and waited until receiving the all clear.

No gunfire was exchanged. If the drug ring or Bree had been there, they were long gone now.

Cecile reappeared and gave them the signal. At that, Lawson and Ashlee finally got out and went inside. Josh was barking orders to the forensic teams to start taking samples.

Bullet holes riddled the far wall, sending beams of sunlight through them and onto the old barn's dirt floor. Fresh footprints were also visible in the dirt. Lawson made sure he trekked around them.

He spotted what looked like brown spots on the ground and carefully knelt to examine them. "Blood," he said, and Josh and Cecile hurried over.

Josh pushed the dirt and found more spots. "Looks like they tried to cover it up." He called over the forensics team to begin gathering evidence while they continued their search.

Ashlee stood by the outside door, reluctant to enter. Her face paled and Lawson thought she must be remembering something. Did being here spark some memory of what she had experienced? It seemed certain she'd been here. Somewhere deep in her subconscious, she knew what had gone down here. She only needed to recall it.

He walked over to her. "You okay? Remembering anything?"

She looked around, anguish on her face as she shook her head. "Nothing is coming back. Something happened here, though, didn't it?"

"It looks that way."

"This is where it happened, whatever it is. This is where it took place."

"More than likely. No one reported hearing any gunfire from here, but this place is so far out and so isolated that it's unlikely anyone would have heard it."

"What does that mean for my sister?" She locked eyes with him.

He didn't know what to say. The only positive he could see was that they hadn't found a body yet—but there was plenty of land just on this property where someone could dump a body and be pretty sure that it wouldn't be found for a long while.

"Should we start a search?" Lawson asked Josh as his brothers and Cecile gathered while the other deputies continued collecting evidence.

Josh nodded. "I'll coordinate it. We need to search all this property." He glanced over at Ashlee, then lowered his voice. "If things went this wrong, we may be looking only to recover a body." Despite his attempt to be discreet, Lawson noticed Ashlee's face pale at his brother's statement.

"I think we should check more into this boyfriend of Bree's," Lawson suggested. "Maybe something in his background can give us some more information. Maybe a location this drug ring might be operating out of."

Colby nodded. "I think Miles has a friend with the DEA. I'll have him call and see if they can read us in on their investigation."

Lawson nodded and thanked him. Sometimes having a brother who was a federal agent was a handy thing.

SEVEN

While the search of the Taylors' abandoned ranch was underway, Lawson drove Ashlee back to Silver Star. She didn't need to be there for the search, mostly because of what they might find, but also because he and Josh and Cecile had deemed it too dangerous for her. There were too many volunteers who had shown up to help search. Members of the drug ring could be hidden among them, watching and waiting for another opportunity to try to abduct her. Returning to the ranch seemed like the right choice.

Ashlee hadn't been happy about leaving, but she hadn't put up too much of a fight over it. She understood the gravity of the situation.

When they arrived at Silver Star, they were greeted by the aroma of fresh pastries. Lawson walked into the kitchen to find one batch cooling on the table while his mother kneaded dough for another.

"Who are all the pastries for?" he asked.

"My ladies' class is sponsoring a bake sale. We're trying to raise funds to sponsor kids to go to summer camp."

"That's nice," Ashlee commented. "Can I help?"

His mother nodded. "Absolutely. You can help me knead this dough."

Ashlee grabbed an apron and jumped right in.

Lawson was glad to see her hands occupied and hoped it would help to take her mind off Bree and the search that was taking place at her old home. He was sure that the need for distraction was the reason for her offer and he couldn't blame her for wanting to keep busy. Too much idle time meant too much opportunity to dwell.

"I want to check on the horses again to make sure they're still okay after yesterday," he announced. "Are you two going to be okay?"

"We'll be fine," his mother said. "But you should be careful. You did just get out of the hospital."

"I'll take it easy. I promise." He paused in the doorway a moment before walking out, enjoying the way Ashlee seemed to be fitting into his life this time around. Funny, he'd never thought that before. Was she finally finding a place here?

Something was different with her. Maybe losing her memory had helped her to get past that obstacle of always overthinking. Maybe she was finally learning to relax and enjoy the simpler things in life—his simpler *way* of life.

Don't get ahead of yourself, Lawson.

Maybe he was seeing just what he wanted to see. This wasn't a vacation. She was traumatized to the point where she had no memory. Whatever had happened to her, she would surely revert back to the way she'd always been once her memories returned.

Was he actually hoping that they never did? He wouldn't want that for her. He wanted her to remember how much they'd once meant to each other. He wanted her to remember the love they'd once shared. Without her memories, he wouldn't be getting Ashlee—the real Ashlee—back.

It was like a stab at his heart that she couldn't remember him. But it hurt more to know that when her memories returned, so would the drive to get away from the ranch—and from him—and return to her fast-paced setup in the city.

What was so important about that life, anyway? Always on the go, the constant pressure. Who wanted that?

He sighed and faced the facts. *Ashlee* wanted that life. She'd chosen it.

Maybe this vacation from herself was her way of admitting she'd tried it and it hadn't been a good fit for her? Wishful thinking again. There he went.

He marched toward the barn, intent on keeping his mind from running in circles. The stables needed to be cleaned and the horses fed, but those chores would have to wait until one of his brothers returned home. Having them around to help was nice, but he normally never minded taking on the extra work alone. This was what he wanted, what he hoped to do full-time once this nightmare with Ashlee was over and his time with the sheriff's department ended. He might still take a shift here and there to help out his brother, but his first love was this ranch and he was dedicated to keeping it going.

He stared at the horses milling about in the pen and the beauty of the land behind them. He took a moment to soak it all in. It reminded him how small his life really was. But it also reminded him that he wanted to be a better person, a person who made a difference in this life.

He'd tried so many things, only to find that all he wanted in life was to be here, tending to this land and to these animals. Admitting that felt like failure. A voice deep inside him kept repeating it was failure. He'd heard it for so long and now he realized the voice belonged to Ashlee. Ashlee telling him he lacked ambition and that he should want more out of life. Her words still followed him around after all these years. He'd always had a clear idea of what he'd wanted out of life until she'd uttered those words—and he'd been doubting himself ever since. Lawson was living his dream but it hadn't seemed like enough.

He'd sought counsel from his father, who'd assured him that ranching was a fine way of life, but still he was struggling to convince himself that that was true. Why did he let the opinions of others sway him so? He tried not to—but this hadn't been just any person. This had been the woman he'd loved and wanted to spend his life with. He'd tried to change for her, but it had never been good enough. It had never been a good fit. No matter what anyone else believed, ranching was his calling. This was the only thing in his life that felt right.

Although, lately, being here with Ashlee had felt right, too, and that was new. While he'd always enjoyed being with her, having her on the ranch had always felt forced before. He'd told himself she would grow to love it, but after she'd run out on him, he'd finally seen the truth. She'd known her way of life wasn't for him. Part of him was glad he hadn't followed her—giving up the ranch to be with her—despite how his heart broke at the end of their relationship. He didn't want a love that felt forced.

God, help me to find my way.

He should be more ambitious and want more out of life. His family wasn't all about the ranch life. His brothers all had careers that were important, that were making a difference in society. Even his sister was in social work, helping people. Who did he help? What value did he offer to the world? He didn't know. It was an issue he'd been struggling with for a long time.

Being a rancher was what Lawson loved—the ranch was where he belonged. But was he imagining it, hoping that his calling was what he loved, or was it true? He'd made so many mistakes and he wasn't sure he was ready to make any more.

What would happen when Ashlee regained her memories? Would she want him back in her life after this time they'd spent together? Would she remember her disdain for this ranch and this town and go back to Dallas like nothing had happened between them? Or was this a new beginning for them? A new future, a second chance to get things right in their relationship?

He hoped so. Either way, he knew one thing for certain. He wasn't letting her walk away from him again. No matter what it meant giving up.

Reassured that the horses were fine, he walked back to the house to check on Ashlee and was greeted at the front door by the aroma of freshly baked goods that made his mouth water. He slipped off his hat and boots and hurried to the kitchen knowing that even when she was baking for others, there were always misshapen pastries his mother would set aside for their family.

He walked into the kitchen and stopped dead in his tracks as he spotted Ashlee at the table sitting across from his mother. But it was what she was eating that sent shock waves through him. She was about to pop a boiled peanut into her mouth and his heart dropped, remembering her allergy. "Ashlee!" He panicked and rushed to her, knocking the offending nut from her hand.

She jumped back. "What are you doing?"

"You're allergic to peanuts."

She stared at the shells of boiled peanuts spread out on the table and her eyes widened as panic crept into them. "I—I didn't know."

His mother stood, her face full of concern. "I'm so sorry. I forgot about that. I should have remembered."

They all should have. They'd been acting like Ashlee was fine, but she wasn't. She was walking around without a filter to know what was right and wrong for her.

He grabbed her arm and rushed her outside. "I've seen you have an allergic reaction before. This is serious. We need to get you to the hospital."

He ushered her to his truck and helped her into the passenger's side, noting how she was already looking pale. He'd seen her swell up once before after ingesting a peanut and it hadn't been a pretty sight. It had nearly killed her that day. Since then, she'd always been incredibly careful about making sure she stayed away from peanut products. Did amnesia take away memories of what she was and wasn't allergic to? Obviously so.

"Are you okay?" he asked as he drove.

She nodded. "I'm okay, but please hurry."

She didn't appear to be swelling up and he thought it would have already happened by now. The best he could remember, she'd started swelling immediately and then it had affected her breathing as she'd experienced anaphylaxis. He floored it, not taking any chances with her health. But he was also keenly watching his surroundings through the mirrors on the truck. He didn't want to be ambushed on the way to the hospital. Ashlee couldn't afford that. Any interruptions could cost her her life.

He roared into town and headed for the medical center. He pulled up in front of the doors and jammed the truck into Park. He wasn't going to waste time hunting down a parking space. He would do that once he knew she was receiving the medical attention she needed.

He rushed around and opened the door for her, noting her face was pale, but she still wasn't showing any signs of swelling. Odd. He didn't wait for her to walk. He swooped her up into his arms and hurried her inside, calling out to the nurse behind the desk that she was having an allergic reaction and needed to be seen. Fortunately, no one else was sitting in the waiting room so the nurse ushered them right to the back.

"Hey, you're going to have to move your truck," a security officer called to him from the front doors.

Lawson checked the instinctive reaction to toss him the keys and tell the guard to do it himself. There was good reason for the rules—hospitals needed to keep their entrances open. The man was only doing his job and Lawson knew a little about how that felt to be hollered and fussed at for upholding regulations from his stint as a deputy sheriff. He even considered playing that card.

"I called the doctor. He'll be right in," the nurse assured him. "She'll be fine until you return."

Finally, he relented as Ashlee also assured him. "I'll be right back," he said before turning on his heel and marching toward the doors. He crawled back into his truck and started the engine, but something was bothering him as he found a parking space.

He was certain she'd swallowed at least a few of those peanuts. Her previous reaction had induced symptoms right away. This time, it had already been at least ten minutes since they'd left the ranch and she wasn't showing a single one of the symptoms he remembered.

He didn't even want to think about what her lack of symptoms indicated.

The doctor shone a light into her eyes, then poked and prodded her. "You don't seem to be having any reaction to the peanuts. How long have you had this allergy and is it severe?"

She shook her head. "I—I don't know. I'm not sure."

He gave her a strange look, then glanced at the chart and nodded understandingly. "It looks like you've recently suffered some loss of memory?"

"Yes, I didn't even know about the allergy until Lawson mentioned it." And she was very sure that she wasn't showing any symptoms, either. True, she didn't know what an allergic reaction felt like—but from Lawson's reaction, it should have been severe, maybe even life-threatening. But she felt fine. And that didn't make any sense. Was it possible he'd been wrong about the allergy? He'd seemed so certain and even his mother, once reminded, recalled that she'd had an allergy to peanuts.

Why, then, wasn't she symptomatic?

Tears filled her eyes as the realization flowed through her. She knew enough to know that amnesia wouldn't take away her allergies to certain things. She could only think of one reason she wasn't swelling up or having trouble breathing.

The doctor kept her under observation for over an hour to make sure she didn't have a delayed reaction, but nothing happened. She continued to be asymptomatic.

When the doctor returned, she questioned him. "Is it possible to stop being allergic to something?"

He shook his head. "Children sometimes outgrow allergies, and with some allergens, it's possible to build up your level of resistance to reduce your symptoms, but it's very unlikely that an allergy would just disappear in an adult. Without knowing the extent of your allergy, it's difficult for me to say for sure. But you're not showing any signs of an allergic reaction, so that's good, right?"

Ashlee wasn't so sure it was a good thing. *Troubling* was a better word.

The doctor handed over her release papers. "Let me know if you have any further problems."

"I will. Thank you."

The nurse came in and held the door. "There's a handsome young man out here itching to see you're okay. Should I tell him to come back?"

"Sure," Ashlee stated, though she wasn't sure she wanted to see Lawson. He wouldn't miss the fact that she wasn't showing symptoms, either. From what he'd said, she knew he'd seen one of her previous attacks first-hand. He was bound to realize that she obviously wasn't in distress.

He walked into the room and slipped off his hat, rubbing at his hat hair before pulling up a chair as she sat on the gurney. "How are you feeling?"

"I'm okay." She didn't elaborate. She didn't want to speculate on why she wasn't having a reaction even though she felt the truth deep inside her. "The doctor says I'm good to go."

He studied her face and then slipped his hat back onto his head as he guarded his eyes from giving away anything he was thinking. She couldn't read him at all. "Let's get you back home."

He led her outside to his pickup and she crawled back onto the seat. They were in the exact same position they'd been in just a little while ago, but as she slipped on the seat belt, she knew something had changed. He'd called the ranch her home and she had grown to believe that, too. It felt like home, like a place she never wanted to leave. But would he still consider her welcome there after tonight?

The silence between them was deafening as he put the truck into Drive and took off, taking it slower this time back to the ranch than he had on the way to the hospital. It was dark out, but she could still make out the landscape passing by, the beautiful country scenery she was coming to love.

Tears slipped from her eyes and she wiped them away.

He gripped the steering wheel, but didn't reach for her hand like he'd done earlier. "It's going to be okay," he told her softly, but she didn't—she couldn't—believe him anymore. Everything had changed.

She didn't belong here and the truth was like a river that flowed between them—one that she couldn't cross. He didn't speak about it and neither did she, yet they knew the truth.

She wasn't Ashlee.

She wasn't the woman he wanted to be with. She was the woman he hadn't a nice word to say about since the day she'd arrived.

She was Bree Taylor.

The wrong twin.

He pulled into the entrance of Silver Star and parked the pickup in front of the house, but he didn't get out right away.

Neither of them had said a word on the drive, but his thoughts had been screaming at him the entire way. She hadn't had a reaction to the peanuts. He could hardly wrap his brain around what that meant.

She sat silently beside him, not hurrying to

get out, either, waiting on him to speak first, but nothing between them was coming as easily as it had only a few hours ago.

"I have some work to do in the barn," he finally said.

She turned to look at him and he sensed she wanted to talk about what this incident meant. But he wasn't in the mood to talk and he wasn't sure what to say, anyhow. Whether she'd meant to or not, she'd deceived him in the worst possible way and now they both knew it.

Finally, she nodded and reached for the handle to open the door. He watched her walk into the house before getting out and heading for the barn. He picked up a shovel and started cleaning out one of the stalls, but it was frustrating and painful work with his injury. His limbs quickly protested and his stitches pulled. Frustration and anger bit at him that he couldn't do the work he needed to do to work out his frustrations and keep him away from whoever that woman was inside his house.

He stopped, took off his hat and rubbed sweat from his forehead before settling it back onto his head. He stared at the house. That wasn't fair. He knew who she was. They both knew it, although he'd not yet allowed himself to accept it.

His gut tightened. If the woman in his house was actually Bree, that meant Ashlee was the one who'd been taken hostage and possibly killed. It shouldn't matter to him which sister had been abducted, but it did. It did matter to him.

He spotted several trucks pull in and park. Moments later, his brothers exited, heading inside. Lawson called out to Josh and hustled over to join him. "What did you find?"

"Nothing so far. I left Deputy Marks in charge of continuing the search, but it's unlikely we'll find anything based on the limited information we have. We'd have to literally stumble over a body at this point."

Given that he now suspected it might be Ashlee out there, Josh's flippant words stabbed at him.

"We will regroup in the morning and reassess." He started to walk off, then turned back. "By the way, Dad called and told me about Ashlee's allergic reaction. I guess you made it to the hospital in time?"

Lawson pulled off his work gloves and twisted them in his hands. "We didn't have to rush. She never had any symptoms."

Josh looked surprised, but Lawson wasn't

sure if that was because of the news—or because of Lawson's wooden tone in delivering it. "That's a good thing…isn't it?" he asked.

He could only shake his head. It was a good thing that she wasn't in danger, but it had left a foul taste in his mouth.

"What are you thinking?" Josh asked him.

"We've been assuming she's Ashlee from the start. How else could we go about making sure that's true?"

"You're having doubts? You think she's lying about her identity?"

No, he didn't think she was lying exactly. "I believe she can't remember—the amnesia seems real. But she only believes she's Ashlee because that's what we've been telling her all along. I just want to make certain we haven't been jumping to conclusions. After all, she does have a twin sister."

"We could try fingerprints," Josh suggested. "It's my understanding that twins don't have identical prints."

Lawson nodded. Bree had a criminal record—her prints would be on file. This question could be answered easily. "Good, let's start there." He hated the doubts that were organizing in his mind, but he couldn't discount them. Logic told him one thing—but his heart protested against it. He couldn't face the fact that he'd been falling for the wrong sister, that he'd been associating memories with a woman who wasn't even there.

He knew Ashlee. Or at least, he thought he did. He'd been so sure it was her. If it wasn't, Bree Taylor was going to have a lot of explaining to do when her memory finally returned. Why had she been in Ashlee's car with her wallet and her identification? And, more important, where was her sister?

Ashlee allowed herself to be fingerprinted by Cecile. She wasn't mad that Lawson had suggested it. In fact, she was anxious to find out the results. After yesterday's events—or lack of events—that suggested she wasn't Ashlee, after all, she was also questioning everything she thought she knew.

As Cecile took each finger and placed it over the computerized pad, Ashlee couldn't help but feel this was familiar, like she'd done this before. For once, a feeling of familiarity bothered her. She wanted clues to her past, but this wasn't a pleasant one to discover. Had she been arrested before? Was she a criminal? This just seemed like more proof that she was Bree rather than Ashlee.

Cecile finished up. "That should do it. I'll

have someone run these through the system and we'll see what comes back."

Ashlee took a seat on the bench outside the interview room and waited. After several minutes, Lawson approached her, but didn't sit beside her like he would have before. He was noticeably nervous, fiddling with his hat as he paced in front of her.

She missed the way he'd once easily slipped in beside her and wrapped his arm around her. She missed the lift of his shoulders when he grinned and the way his blue eyes glowed when he looked at her.

She closed her eyes at the realization that those days were over. The comfort and support he offered were more than likely things her sister would get to experience again, but not her, and she hated the way she longed to have him wrap his arms around her one more time and assure her everything was going to be okay.

Time seemed to drag as they waited, until finally Lawson's phone buzzed at his hip. He took it out and glanced at the screen before taking a deep breath and putting it away.

"She's ready for us."

He slipped his hat back onto his head. Ashlee stood, taking a deep breath of her own before bracing herself for what was to come, and marched toward the back of the sheriff's office.

Cecile led them inside an interview room.

"You have the results?" Lawson queried once they sat down.

"I do," she stated.

"What's the verdict?" he asked and Ashlee felt her heart race. Was she ready to hear this? And what would happen if these prints proved she was in fact Bree and not Ashlee? She didn't know, but there was no turning back now.

Cecile hit a key on the computer and an image popped up on the screen. It was a photo of either her or her sister, and both she and Lawson leaned in to see the name beside it.

"Ashlee Taylor." Lawson's breath caught as he read the name then the charges. "Arrested in Dallas three years ago for drug possession. Looks like the charges were dismissed, but the prints remained in the system." Lawson glanced at her and she suddenly felt on the spot by his accusatory glare before he turned his focus back to Cecile. "They're identical twins. Is it possible they have identical fingerprints?"

Cecile shook her head. "When you asked about doing this, I had the same question. I've never run across a similar situation, so I did some research. Fingerprints aren't merely the result of genetic makeup. They're formed in the womb and can be influenced by several factors such as blood pressure, bone growth and even nutrition. Therefore, they may be similar, but no two people have identical fingerprints, not even twins." She motioned to the points of matching. "A fingerprint match has to have several identifying characteristics shared with the ones we've run before they're considered a match. In this case, all of the points match. These prints belong to the same person. There's no doubt about that."

Ashlee took a deep breath. This wasn't the outcome she'd expected. The drug charge was concerning, but the name attached to it was downright shocking. According to her prints, she was Ashlee Taylor. But wasn't she supposed to be the more responsible sister? How did a drug charge work into that? This entire situation had just been made all the more complicated.

Lawson stared at her until she squirmed under his gaze. "Stop looking at me like that," she demanded. "I'm as surprised as you are."

"This doesn't make any sense."

"What doesn't make sense? That I'm Ashlee, after all? Or that I'm not the perfect woman you remembered me to be?" The wounded expression on his face told her that her words had hit their mark. She hadn't meant to be so mean about it, but they'd both needed to face the truth. He'd been imagining her as someone she wasn't and could never be.

He sighed. "I guess I have sort of placed you up on a pedestal, haven't I?"

"You keep saying we had this picture-perfect relationship, but if that's the truth, then why did I leave? Something wasn't right or we would be married today, wouldn't we?"

He nodded, but rubbed his face. "I'll give you that, Ashlee, but this drug charge doesn't make any sense. I could understand if Bree was arrested for possession, but not you."

"I don't understand it, either, but I don't have an explanation. I guess I've changed a lot since you knew me. Six years is a long time."

He shook his head, unwilling to believe she'd fallen so far. "Not that long."

Cecile put up her hands to stop their bickering. "Wait, there's more." She hit another key and another mug shot appeared, also her, but the name that popped up with it was Bree Taylor.

They both looked at her, confused.

"What does this mean?" Lawson asked Cecile.

"The prints captured another match. Bree Taylor's."

Ashlee sucked in a breath. Her fingerprints matched prints recorded in the system for both Ashlee and Bree? "I thought you said twins didn't have identical fingerprints."

"They don't. I might expect both sisters' prints to pop up just because of the similar points of matching. But, in this case, *all* points match both sets of prints."

"What does that mean?" Lawson asked Cecile.

"It means the prints on file for both Ashlee and Bree were made by the same person. Without additional evidence, we can't say whose is whose. These tests are just inconclusive."

Lawson again trained his stare on Ashlee and she squirmed. It wasn't the conclusive evidence they'd wanted, but it seemed to be yet another point checked off in the not-Ashlee column. She was more and more convinced she was not Ashlee Taylor. But that still didn't answer the more pressing question.

Where was her sister?

Ashlee and Lawson returned to the ranch, the cab of the truck once again silent as they drove. At any moment, she expected Lawson to toss her out of the truck for being a fraud. And she wouldn't blame him if he did. The truth was, she wished he would say something to give her a clue about where his mind was—even if it meant yelling at her. Anything was better than the silence between them.

He parked in front of the house, but didn't get out.

"Let me guess, you have chores to do in the barn." He'd used that excuse to keep himself busy and away from her several times now and it was getting old.

"That's right, I do. This ranch doesn't run itself. It takes a lot of work."

His defensive tone made her cringe. She didn't doubt there was work to be done, but he had always found time to be with her during her first few days on the ranch. The timing right now made it clear that chores were being used as a good enough excuse to stay away from her.

She got out and walked onto the porch just as the door swung open and his mother met her. "Hi, Ashlee. This was delivered for you." She handed Ashlee a box labeled with her name. She wasn't expecting a package and who would know she was staying here anyway? The only scenario to explain it was that maybe Jake Stephens had finally caved and sent her the client files they'd requested. Reassured that must be what was in the box, she thanked Diane, then hurried upstairs to the bedroom and tore open the package. She wasn't even sure she should be opening it since it was meant for Ashlee and… Well, she wasn't sure she should open it. She probably wouldn't even know what she was looking at, but she still needed to take a look before handing them over to Lawson and Josh.

If she knew for certain she was Bree and not Ashlee, it would explain why seeing Jake Stephens had had no effect on her.

Chalk one more up for the not-Ashlee column.

The files she'd expected weren't inside the box. Instead, she found a cell phone, a DVD with the words *Watch Me* written on the plastic case, and a typewritten note.

Return what Travis took from us if you want to see your sister alive again. We'll contact you with a location. Come alone or Bree is dead.

She gasped and realized this was a second ransom demand. They were giving her another opportunity to bring her sister home. She booted up the old desktop computer on Kellyanne's desk and popped in the DVD.

The screen flickered, then a video image appeared. Ashlee gasped and covered her mouth in horror. The image was of her sister tied to a chair, tape covering her mouth and bruises on her face. A newspaper was taped to the front of her shirt. Tears filled her sister's eyes as a voice off camera barked orders at her after pulling off the tape.

"Speak," growled a rough voice from behind the camera.

"This message is for my sister Ashlee. They're including this paper so you can see I'm still alive. However, they assure me that I won't be for long unless you return what Travis took from these men. They've included a burner cell phone in the envelope. They'll send you a text message with the meeting place. They don't want a repeat of what happened before. Come alone or they will kill me."

Ashlee stared at her sister's image. Tears began to stream down her face at her sister's plight.

"I'm sorry, sis. I'm sorry for putting you in this situation. These guys mean business. They want what Travis took from them." She choked over her words before continuing. "You never should have been put in the middle of this. I'm so sorry."

The image disappeared and Ashlee cried out and reached for the computer screen, but it was blank.

Sobs racked her and she fell to the floor as she realized what must have happened. They'd mistaken Ashlee for her, they'd kidnapped the wrong twin in an effort to get back at Travis. She wiped away tears, her first instinct to go to Lawson and show him this video.

She stopped before she even got to her feet.

He would insist on turning the video over to his brother. The cell phone, too. Not to mention, Josh and the others would never allow her to return the money to the kidnappers.

Getting her sister back alive had to be her one and only priority. She couldn't risk it by not following their instructions. They'd told her to come alone and that was just what she was going to do.

The package had been addressed to Ashlee and her sister had called her by that name—that meant she hadn't told them anything. They didn't yet know they had kidnapped the wrong twin.

She shut down the computer and slipped the cell phone into her pocket. She had to do this alone, knowing that it was the last thing

Lawson, Josh and the others would advise her to do. But Lawson would thank her once this was all done and she'd returned his Ashlee to him, reuniting him with his one true love.

She stood and walked to the window, catching sight of him outside the barn. He'd told her he was falling for her, but he'd been fooled into believing she was someone else when he'd said that. She couldn't hold him to those words. They'd been spoken when he'd believed she was someone else. If he'd known she was Bree and not Ashlee, he would never have said them, never even would have considered expressing those feelings for her.

Seeing her sister on that video had shaken something loose inside her. Maybe it was the shock of seeing Ashlee that way and knowing for certain that she was in danger. Maybe it was the difference between looking at a picture and having video, hearing her voice. For whatever reason, memories were beginning to return—jarring and incomplete, but there. She wiped away the tears as they flowed and knew what she had to do.

She still wasn't sure why they had her or what she'd done to get into this situation, but she would do whatever it took to rescue her sister from these people. She didn't even know who to trust...except for Lawson, whom she trusted completely. But she couldn't risk her sister's life on the captors' dangerous games.

She was going to get her sister back even if she had to take her place or die doing so. And that meant doing it alone, without Lawson or his brothers interfering.

But first she had to figure out a way to get her hands on the money.

EIGHT

With nothing to do but wait, Lawson continued taking out his frustrations by cleaning the stalls. His mind was rolling over and over the situation and the options seemed bleak. While the fingerprint situation confused things on the surface, he was pretty sure they all believed that it was Bree with them, not Ashlee. He could just see Bree getting arrested and giving her name as Ashlee, leading to those prints ending up in the system under the wrong name. This meant they still didn't know where the real Ashlee was. Wherever she was, she was in trouble. That much was obvious to anyone with two eyes. Bree's actions had brought down a world of trouble on her sister.

He took some comfort in the physical work even though it was a struggle, but couldn't shut off his brain or stop himself from trying to fix the situation. Why would God give him a desire for a simple, physical life as a rancher when he needed to be skilled in law enforcement to save Ashlee from a drug ring? He didn't understand it and so far, God wasn't responding to his questions.

"Hi."

The voice from behind him stopped him, but he quickly got himself together and continued to work. He couldn't deal with her right now. He wasn't ready for that. Why hadn't she just remained inside and left him alone?

He ran a sleeve across his forehead to wipe away the sweat that was flowing. "What do you want?"

"We should really talk about this, Lawson."

He knew she was right—but he wasn't ready for that conversation. "Now isn't a good time." His brain was still trying to find a way to work through all of this. Patience and determination were the answers. They always were, but mustering either one right now had him stumped. He'd never thought much of Bree in the past, but he had to admit he'd never really taken the time to get to know her before, either. Now, during her time here on the ranch, he'd grown to care about her more than he wanted to admit.

He heard her footsteps approaching. All he

wanted from her was distance while he figured this thing out, but she wasn't even going to give him that.

"Lawson, please." She touched his shoulder and he shuddered.

Her touch still had the power to do that and he hated it. An angry, hurting part of him hissed that she'd drawn him in, tricked him into falling for her, let him believe she was someone else. He knew he wasn't being fair—for starters, he truly believed her amnesia was real—but he couldn't be bothered about fairness just now.

"Can't we talk about this? Let me explain."

He turned to her and saw differences now, things he'd been blind not to see before. He'd chosen to ignore the clues that she wasn't who she'd said she was. "What do you mean you want to explain? Have you started to remember?"

She shrugged. "It's coming back, a little at a time. Not how I ended up in that car or where they're holding her, but who I am, my past."

He tossed the shovel against the wall and slipped off his gloves and hat, slinging them away, too, as he confronted her. "Your past. So you remember why your prints came up as Ashlee's?"

Her face reddened and she lowered her head. But he was determined now to make her face up to what she'd done. Maybe if Ashlee had held Bree accountable for her actions back in the past, they wouldn't be in this mess now. "No, don't look away. You wanted to talk, so let's talk. I want to know why those prints came back as your sister's."

She glanced up at him, resignation in her face. "Because I used Ashlee's name once when I was arrested. I said I was her and they believed me. They eventually figured it out, but I guess it was never fixed in the system."

He'd figured as much but, at the confirmation, anger washed over him again. "You pretended to be her then just like you're doing now."

"I wasn't pretending, Lawson. I promise you. I didn't know. I never meant to deceive you. I certainly never meant for Ashlee to get hurt, even though I know you blame me for landing her in this situation."

"Who else is there to blame? Your ex-boyfriend who decided to overdose instead of saving your sister's life?"

"I've made mistakes. Travis was a mistake, a huge mistake, but I had left him before all of this happened. I was trying to get my life together. Ashlee was helping me."

He picked up a rake and leaned against it. "And look where that got her." He turned away and started raking up one of the stalls. He didn't like letting his anger release, but he'd needed to say those things. He couldn't look at her, because the truth was that he had started to care about this woman—not just as Ashlee, but as herself. In all honesty, he'd come to appreciate all the little things that were different from Ashlee. He'd liked her nurturing touch and her eagerness to help. She had the ability to live in the moment and laugh without the need to strive for perfection. He'd liked that, too. It was so unlike the Ashlee he remembered that he couldn't believe he hadn't seen the differences. And whether it was true or not, it felt like she'd tricked him into falling for her.

"I can't change what's happened," she said. "All I can do is say I'm sorry and try to make it better."

"There's nothing you can do. Leave this one to the professionals."

"I don't know if Ashlee ever told you or not, but our parents used to fight all the time. It often got very frightening, especially when we were kids. There were a couple of times when our mom was helping your mom with some church stuff that I came here with her to Silver Star. I remember how peaceful it was. I felt safe here then. I think that's why this place felt so familiar to me when I first arrived."

He didn't recall them ever coming to the ranch, but he'd been young then, too, and probably had forgotten. But her words about their parents stung because Ashlee hadn't told him about their fighting. He was beginning to realize there was so much she hadn't shared with him.

"I'm going to bring her home to you, Lawson," she told him. "I promise I'll make it right."

He was glad when she turned and left. He didn't want to acknowledge the sincerity in her voice any more than he wanted to acknowledge the draw he still felt toward her. He wanted to remain angry, to hold on to that bitterness. It was the only thing that was keeping him going.

She had to act fast. That cell phone in her pocket could ring at any time and she had to be ready. After brainstorming ways to get her hands on the money the sheriff's office had confiscated, she'd determined it wasn't possible so she'd had to come up with a plan B.

Now to execute it before that phone rang with the ransom demand and she ran out of time.

She walked back into the house and feigned a headache in front of his mother before telling her she was going upstairs to rest. The woman gave her a knowing look and Bree was certain Diane knew she was faking the headache, but she probably thought Bree was doing it because she needed time away from Lawson.

She locked the door to the bedroom, then pulled out the fire escape ladder she'd found under Kellyanne's bed, positioning it toward the window. She sat and watched the barn, silently praying for Lawson to hurry up and go inside. She couldn't act until she was certain he was out of the way.

She shouldn't have tried to see him one last time. That had been a mistake. He would never forgive her for not being Ashlee, but if her plan worked, he would soon be reunited with the woman he loved.

Bree didn't yet remember all of the circumstances of the canceled engagement, but she was sure that once Ashlee and Lawson were reunited, they'd find a way to overcome the past. It was clear Lawson still loved Ashlee, and he deserved to have everything he wanted. And as for her sweet sister… Ashlee deserved nothing but the best. And that was Lawson, no question.

The phone buzzed in her pocket and her heart stopped. She pulled it out and looked at it, glad to see the message wasn't from the kidnappers, not yet. She still had time. She texted her coconspirator that she would be there to meet him soon.

Finally, Lawson entered the house. She heard the front door slam, then the sound of his footsteps on the stairs as he went to his bedroom or possibly to shower. This was her time to act. She carefully lowered the ladder so that it made almost no sound, then climbed down to the ground and hurried to the barn.

Careful to not alert anyone, Bree.

She quickly saddled up the horse she'd ridden before and led it outside. She was fortunate most of the family was gone this afternoon, but that still meant she had to be careful to sneak away without being seen or heard by Lawson or his mom. Both were inside the house. She led the horse to the back of the barn and caught a reflection of herself in the window. This woman she'd become here at Silver Star was the woman she wanted to be—but that life was gone from her now. She climbed onto the horse and it led her away from the barn. She would circle around to the road once she knew she wouldn't be seen.

She reached the end of the field by the back gate and turned back to look. No one was coming after her. She'd made a clean get-away, but it wouldn't take long before Lawson realized one of the horses was missing. He would certainly notice that before he noticed she was gone.

Once she was in an open field, she pushed the horse into a gallop and hurried toward the road. It didn't take long to find a silver car waiting for her. She slid off the horse, crawled under a bar on the split-rail fence and walked up the embankment to the road.

The driver's door opened and Jake Stephens got out. He ran to her, sweeping her up into his arms. "Ashlee! I'm so glad you called."

She let him hug her, but didn't return his embrace, which he didn't seem to notice. She *did* stop him when he tried to kiss her.

"Did you bring the money?"

He pulled away, then walked to the car and handed her a bag. She unzipped it and saw stacks of bills.

"Twenty-five thousand dollars. It wasn't easy to get in cash so quickly. That's a lot of money, Ashlee. Are you going to tell me now why you need it?"

She stood to face him. She had kind of pulled him into her scheme under false pretenses. It was time to come clean. "I'm not Ashlee. I'm her sister, Bree. Ashlee is in trouble. She's been kidnapped. The money I was found with was her ransom money, but the police confiscated it."

His eyes widened in shock. "Surely, they'll release it if you need it to rescue her."

"No, I can't tell the police what I'm planning—and you can't tell anyone, either. I know these people who are holding Ashlee captive. They'll kill her if I don't do as they say."

He stared at her for several long seconds. "Well, I'm coming with you."

"I can't allow that. They told me to come alone. If they see someone with me…"

He nodded grimly. "They'll kill her."

"Yes." She saw the confusion and worry in his face. It was obvious he truly cared for her sister. "I will get her back, I promise. Give me your keys, then wait at the hotel until you hear from me."

He handed the key ring over and she hopped into his car. Tears rolled down her cheeks as she sped down the road, and she wiped them away. There was no use crying over how she'd never see Lawson again. All that mattered now was getting to the kidnappers and getting her sister back safely. It didn't matter what happened to her. Ashlee was the good one, the one everyone loved and cared for. She deserved to live a safe, happy life. Meanwhile, Bree was the one who'd gotten them all into this mess. She couldn't escape her past. She'd been a fool to ever believe she could. No matter what she did, she would always be the one who'd endangered them all.

She glanced at Jake in the rearview mirror. He could find his own way back to the hotel. She had the money. Now she only needed to know where to take it.

A text message instructed her to drive to Milner's Grocery Store and wait for further instructions. She glanced in the rearview mirror. No one was following her. Did the Averys even know she was gone yet? In this case, Lawson's cold shoulder worked in her favor, but she couldn't resist typing a text message to him telling him how sorry she was for everything and asking his forgiveness.

Not just for the last few days, but for all the

years in the past that had dragged his opinion of her so low.

It was more than she deserved, but she hoped for his sake that he could forgive her. She didn't want him to carry the burden of bitterness and anger after she was gone.

Once she pulled into the parking lot, she was dead. It was only a matter of time until the deed was done and she was only existing until then.

She'd told him about why she'd felt safe at the ranch, but she hadn't shared why he'd seemed so familiar to her even without her memories. She'd been enamored with him since the first day she'd stepped foot on Silver Star as a child. She'd fallen off a fence while playing and he'd rushed over to help her, igniting a schoolgirl crush that hadn't faded even when he'd started dating her sister.

She pulled into the grocery store lot and parked under the streetlamp as instructed. At the side of the building, headlights came on and a car pulled forward, stopping alongside her. She hit Send on the text message, then reached for the bag with the money, locked the doors and got out, dropping the keys onto the ground beside the car. The back door of the other car opened and a man got out. "Did you come alone?" he demanded, flashing a glimpse of the gun tucked into his belt.

"Yes. This isn't a trick. I only want my sister returned safely." She was alone, truly all alone.

"What's in the bag?"

She held it out to him and he jerked it from her hand and opened the case, then motioned for her to get into the backseat.

"Where's my sister?"

"She's with the boss. Everything goes right, you'll both be home in time for supper."

She didn't believe him, but she didn't have a choice but to comply. They'd promised to release Ashlee and she was holding them to that. Whatever happened to her happened. She had no illusions about making it out of this mess alive.

She crawled into the backseat. The man shoved at her when she didn't move quickly enough and she bit back a retort about how she was moving as fast as she could. She had to play it safe until she found Ashlee, until she ensured her sister's survival and release.

The driver put the car into gear and took off.

Bree glanced back at the rental car and silently whispered a goodbye to Lawson and the future she'd been hoping to have with him.

* * *

Lawson exited the house after supper and went out to do the final night checks on the horses. Ashlee had stayed upstairs in her room. His mom had said she'd been upset when she'd come inside earlier, and shame had filled him. He'd been too rough with her, taken out his frustrations over this entire mess on her.

He didn't blame her. He wanted to, but he knew as well as anyone how someone's past could come back to bite them. If he was truthful with himself, he was more mad that he'd allowed himself to fall for her without realizing she wasn't Ashlee. He'd chosen to ignore all the contradictions, wanting to believe that Ashlee had changed—that things were different now. But of course they were different. She was a different person.

One that he'd come to care about despite himself. His memories of Bree weren't all bad. When they were younger, she'd had an easy smile and a kindness about her that he still saw. And she'd always been the one to see the best in others.

He walked out to bring the horses in from the pen, but noticed one of them was missing. He walked into the barn, but the mare wasn't in the stable, either—and he noticed one of the saddles was gone, too. Someone had taken out the horse.

He reached for his cell phone to call his brothers to find out if one of them had taken her, but spotted a message on his phone from a number he didn't recognize. He hadn't heard it come through and realized his ringer was off. He opened the message and his blood ran cold.

Forgive me for everything, Lawson. I had to do this. I'll bring her home to you. Bree.

He hurried inside and upstairs to Kellyanne's room. The door was locked, but no one responded when he knocked. He didn't hear her moving around inside.

"No, no, no." He kicked open the door just as Colby and Paul ascended the stairs.

"Everything okay?" Paul asked.

Lawson glanced around the room. She wasn't there and the emergency ladder was hanging from the window. He glanced down, but she wasn't anywhere in sight.

"What's going on?" Colby asked as he and Paul stood in the doorway.

He took a long breath as he tried to process what was happening and what she'd done. She'd sneaked out on him, gone off on her own to rescue her sister and left him with only this text message as to where to find her. "It's Bree. She's missing."

His brothers looked at one another. "Don't you mean Ashlee?" Paul asked, and Lawson didn't know whether to laugh or cry.

"That's a whole conversation in itself," he told his brothers. "All I know is that she's gone. She sent me a text from a number I don't recognize that said she was going to bring her sister home."

He held out his phone so they could see the message. Both their jaws tightened. They all knew this wasn't good news.

"Now, hold on," Paul said. "She wouldn't have left to track down her sister on her own—she'd know that you have better resources than anything she could manage by herself. If she left, then it means she knew where to go. Someone told her—and I'm guessing it was the same person who gave her whatever number she's texting from."

His brother was right. "Mom said she got a package in the mail. Said it was from her office, but I don't see any files." He picked up the keyboard and a sheet of paper beneath it fell from the desk. He bent to scoop it up, already noticing typewritten words that indicated a ransom letter.

He handed it to Colby who read it. Noticing an empty CD-ROM sleeve sitting next to the computer, Lawson booted up the machine and opened the video file on the disk. He watched the recording and his heart dropped.

The kidnappers had sent another ransom letter and Bree had gone to rescue her sister alone.

She'd sneaked away to hand herself over to a drug ring.

"So, let me get this straight. Ashlee isn't Ashlee? She's Bree, Ashlee's twin sister?" Paul gave him a confused stare.

Lawson shot his brother a frustrated look. "Her identical twin sister, yes."

"And how long have you known?"

He gave a half-hearted shrug, but didn't answer. He was trying to keep his thoughts focused on Ashlee and getting her back safely. He'd seen the fear written in her eyes in the video and it had shaken him. But he was surprised to find that his concern for Ashlee was nothing compared to his terror at the thought of the danger Bree was facing.

He wanted to remain angry at her and he was, but his strongest feelings were worries for her safety and panic over the thought of losing her, too. She'd not only sneaked out on him to go rescue her sister, she'd also sneaked her way into his life, becoming the woman he wanted to get to know better.

First, he had to find her.

Josh's phone rang and he scooped it up. "You're on speaker," Josh told Cecile as they all gathered around to hear what she'd found out about the cell phone number Bree had sent the text from. "Tell me you have good news."

"Some. The phone was activated two days ago and received an incoming text an hour ago."

"Any chance we know what that text said?" Colby asked her.

"No, we only have a record of it arriving, but not what it said."

"Probably directions to the handoff," Lawson said and his brothers nodded their agreement.

"What about GPS?" Paul asked.

"GPS is not active, so we can't track it. However, here's something interesting. The phone also made an outgoing call earlier this afternoon. You'll never guess to whom—Jake Stephens."

"I thought we ruled him out as involved in this," Colby stated, and Josh shook his head.

"Well, he just jumped right back into the mix."

Cecile continued. "I pulled his credit card information and he just checked into the Sanderson Hotel and this morning made a twenty-five-thousand-dollar withdrawal from his accounts."

"He's giving her the money," Lawson stated. "To replace the money we have in custody."

"Thanks, Cecile," Josh said. "We're heading over to the hotel now to have a conversation with Mr. Stephens."

Lawson glanced at him as he ended the call. They'd never completely ruled out Jake Stephens being the threat against Ashlee, but it didn't make sense he would withdraw the very amount of money Bree had supposedly taken from the ring. "You think he's involved?" he asked his brother.

"I don't know, but he's the only lead we have right now. Maybe he can tell us where she's headed."

Lawson drew his weapon and took his position on the left side of the hotel door. The manager had given them a key card to Stephens's room. Josh and Colby took positions on the other side. Lawson entered the key card, waited for the green light, then he pushed open the door and they rushed inside.

"Courtland County Sheriff, freeze," Josh hollered.

Jake Stephens was dressed, but stretched out on the bed when they rushed inside. At their entrance, he leaped up and raised his hands.

"What's going on?" he asked as Colby checked the bathroom and Josh the closet before announcing them both clear.

"Where's Ashlee?" Lawson demanded, keeping his weapon raised. He didn't call her by her true name because he figured that would only confuse Stephens, who still believed she was his Ashlee.

"She's been kidnapped. Can you believe that?"

"You spoke to her this morning and you withdrew twenty-five thousand from your bank account. What was that money for?"

"She asked me for it. She said it would help her sister. Only, when I got there to pick her up, the woman waiting for me wasn't Ashlee. It was her sister, Bree."

"You saw her, then," Lawson said. "Where?"

"Just outside the turnoff to your ranch. I thought I was helping my girlfriend. Now, I don't know if I've been scammed or not. Maybe she took that money and left town."

Lawson lowered his gun and holstered it. Jake Stephens's story seemed to make sense. "You didn't get scammed. Ashlee really was kidnapped. We found the ransom note and video of her that the kidnappers sent to Bree. They must have grabbed Ashlee believing she was her sister."

"You said you picked her up," Colby interjected. "Where did you take her?"

"I didn't take her anywhere. In fact, she grabbed my keys and took off in my car. I had to call a cab just to get back here."

Josh reached for his phone. "Your car have GPS?"

"It's a rental car, so yeah."

Josh hit redial on his phone and waited until Cecile answered. "I need to know the GPS coordinates of Jake Stephens's rental car. And send a deputy to bring Stephens back to the office. I want to know where he is at all times until this is over."

Colby placed a hand on Lawson's shoulder. "Don't worry, little brother. We'll get your lady back."

He felt better hearing his brother sound so certain, but he was also concerned because he didn't know which lady Colby had been referring to.

Or even which one Lawson was more worried about getting back.

The car turned off on the entrance road to an old abandoned ranch that used to belong to the Tillman family. They pulled past the house and stopped in front of the garage. The back door opened and Bree was shoved out of the car and led inside.

The man leading her didn't stop, dragging her toward the back to a storage room that he unlocked with a key. When he opened the door, Bree spotted her sister huddled in the corner. She fell nearly on top of Ashlee, but grabbed her and pulled her into a hug, noting the bruises on her face and her busted lip. Those were new since the video had been made.

"Ashlee!"

Her sister clung to her as sobs shook her body. Finally, Ashlee calmed enough to speak. "I never thought I would see you again. Why did you come here? What were you thinking?"

"I had to come. I couldn't let you take the fall for this."

"You were out. Why did you come back?"

Bree stroked her hair, pushing it from her face. "I couldn't leave you here to die."

Ashlee pulled Bree to her. "I was so worried about you when you showed up with the money and then the shooting started." A tear slipped from her swollen eye. "I didn't know if you were dead or alive. It wasn't until they forced me to make that video that I realized you must have made it out. What happened?"

"Lawson Avery happened. He found me, Ashlee. He rescued me in every way a person can be rescued." She pulled off her sister's binds. "There's only one problem. He thought I was you." Ashlee locked eyes with her, looking shocked, and Bree felt her face redden. "I didn't mean to deceive him. After I left you here, I was so traumatized that I had some kind of mental break. I passed out on the side of the road and when I woke up, I had amnesia. I couldn't remember my own name or what I was doing here. Lawson was the one who was there when I woke up. As soon as he saw me, he assumed I was you—and it seemed to be true when we realized I was driving your car and had your billfold with your identification. I never meant to lie to him."

Ashlee pushed away her tears. "I believe you, Bree. I'm sure he will, too."

"I brought the same amount of money Travis took. They promised they would let you go if I returned it."

Ashlee's fingers dug into her arms. "They don't want the money, Bree. They want something else Travis took from them. A notebook of some kind. Do you remember it?"

Bree tried to recall ever seeing something like that around Travis's apartment, but she was coming up blank. There were still big, gaping holes in her memory. "I don't remember anything like that. But wait, this doesn't make any sense. Why would they ask for the money if they really wanted a notebook?"

Ashlee shrugged. "Maybe they thought he kept the notebook with the money? If the info in that notebook is important, then I doubt they'd want you to look too closely at it. Saying they wanted the money would be a demand you wouldn't question—and you'd have no reason to go digging through the bag."

"They were wrong either way," Bree replied. "The notebook wasn't with the money—and this isn't the same money Travis took, anyway. The police confiscated that. I had to get the money elsewhere. There's nothing in the bag I gave them other than cash."

"Then they won't let us go. Either of us." Ashlee was nearly hysterical with fear.

Bree didn't blame her after what she'd been

through, but she knew they both had to remain calm and coolheaded if she was going to be able to get her sister out of this mess alive.

"They will, Ashlee. I'll make sure of it." Her statement held more bravado than actual certainty, but it seemed to calm Ashlee down a bit.

Bree sat with her sister and tried to think of a way out of this mess she'd created.

Why had she waited so long to realize that Travis's addiction would always control his life? If she'd realized it sooner, maybe she—they—wouldn't be in this mess. No, she wasn't responsible for what Travis had done. She'd tried to do the right thing in the end. She had to hold on to that. She'd tried to make a change for the better.

She was just sorry, so sorry, that Ashlee had gotten caught in the middle of her mess.

A verse from the Bible floated to her mind. She remembered it from her days of Sunday school, but she'd heard it recently from Diane Avery's reading it aloud. Something about there being no condemnation for those who loved and believed in Jesus Christ.

Bree nearly laughed at the concept. What would it be like to not be judged by her past mistakes, to find true forgiveness and freedom? To find love and build a life with someone… Someone like Lawson? She shook her head. That was out of the question and it was time she stopped thinking about him. She would never see him again. Even if she managed to somehow live through this nightmare, Lawson Avery would never give her the time of day again after the danger she'd brought to her sister's doorstep.

Lawson rode with Colby to the grocery store where the GPS had pinged the location of the rental car while Josh returned to his office to connect with Cecile. The rental was in the lot, parked beneath a streetlamp. Lawson hopped out and ran to it. The door was locked, but he spotted the keys on the ground beneath it. He quickly opened the door and looked inside. Bree was gone and so was the money Stephens said he'd given her, but the cell phone was lying on the seat. He opened it and read the text that instructed her to get into a waiting vehicle.

Frustration bit at him and he resisted the urge to toss the cell phone across the car. "She's not here," he told his brother. "And the trail has gone cold. They had a car waiting. She must have gotten into it."

Why had she gone off like that? Why hadn't she told him and waited for him and his brothers to come up with a plan? She was too stubborn and determined for her own good. He rubbed his face and tried to calm his frustration and irritation. Of course, she was stubbornly determined to rescue her sister. He couldn't really fault her for that.

"Calm down," Colby said, coming up behind him. "We'll find her. Someone must have seen something. She can't have been gone long. Let's start canvasing the area. You start in the parking lot. I'll go inside the store."

Lawson agreed and watched his brother walk briskly into the store. Once again, he was glad to have cooler heads prevailing because his mind was flailing, looking for some sense of order, ever since he'd realized Bree was gone.

He understood that she wanted to help her sister—of course he understood that. But the fact that she hadn't come to him for help... he could only see one explanation for it. She didn't trust him to find her sister. It was that plain and simple. She didn't think he had what it took to pull this off. Just like Ashlee, Bree didn't believe he was good enough.

When Ashlee had called him unambitious before she'd walked out of his life, he'd been paralyzed with doubt. He couldn't allow that to happen now. Both sisters' lives depended on his finding them and bringing them home safely. And he would do that, no matter what Bree Taylor thought of him. He wasn't going to show her she was wrong about him as some way of proving himself. He didn't need to do that. But he was going to find her and bring her home safely because he couldn't imagine living without her.

Whoa. Where had that thought come from?

Since when could he no longer imagine living without Bree?

He didn't know how it had happened, but that woman had managed to worm her way into his heart. She wasn't the same woman he'd thought he'd known all those years ago. He'd judged her too harshly for her past mistakes. Thinking about what he'd said to her when he'd thought she was Ashlee made his heart sink. He had to get her back if for nothing more than to apologize and to let her know he'd been wrong about her. Bree was more than her past mistakes and he needed to ask for her forgiveness for his narrow-mindedness.

Lawson approached several people in the parking lot, showing Bree's photo and asking if they had seen her, but no one had. He had no idea how long ago it had been since she'd been here. He was ashamed to admit he had no idea how long she'd been gone before they'd realized she was missing, but, according to Jake Stephens, it had already been several hours since she'd taken his car. Anyone who had seen her coming and going might have been gone from the store by now.

He spotted a man and woman loading groceries into their car and jogged over to them, deciding to take one last chance before calling it quits. "I wonder if you've seen this woman?" he asked, showing them her photo on his cell phone.

The woman glanced at the picture, then nodded. "Yes, we saw her when we arrived. She was sitting in that car." She pointed to the rental car. "As we were walking into the store, I saw her get out and get into another car with two men."

"You didn't happen to notice the license plate of the car she got into, did you?"

"No, sorry, but it was a black SUV."

"How long ago was this?"

She glanced at her husband. "About an hour?" Her husband nodded in agreement.

He thanked them for their help, then spotted the security cameras aimed at the parking lot and hurried into the store. Maybe the manager could give them access to that security feed.

He met up with his brother who'd had the same idea and was already in the store's office with another man. "This is Bob Lewis, the manager on duty. He's pulling up the security feed for us now."

The manager scrolled back through the video images until Lawson spotted Bree.

"There," he said, pointing to the figure by the streetlamp as she got out of the rental car and into an SUV.

"Can you get an image of that license plate?" Colby asked and Lewis was able to stop the video so they could see the plate clearly displayed. "You have an excellent video surveillance system, Mr. Lewis. Especially for such a small store."

Lewis shrugged. "My son-in-law sells security systems, so he got me a good price and did the installation himself. Times are hard and crime has become a problem. I believe it's important to keep my customers safe if I want to stay in business."

Lawson and Colby thanked him, then walked out and Lawson texted the info to Josh to get him to run the plates.

Josh had an answer for them by the time they returned to the sheriff's office. "The car is registered to a company called Strategic Design Systems. Supposedly, they manufacture software."

Lawson frowned. He'd been expecting to find a person at the end of this trail, not a corporation. "I've never heard of it."

"Its official address is in Atlanta. But here's the thing. When I ran the plates, they brought up a whole bunch of red flags."

"What kind of flags?"

"DEA flags," Josh stated. "I'm waiting to hear back from a friend at the DEA, but from what I can gather, Strategic Design Systems might be a shell company for a major drug distribution ring."

Lawson took off his hat and pulled a hand through his hair. Bree and Ashlee's captors were major players and that just made getting the sisters both back even more dangerous.

"Hang on," Cecile said, digging through a stack of files.

"What is it?" Josh asked.

"That name—Strategic Design Systems… I know I've seen it before." She dug through a file, then nodded. "We canvased some of the businesses around town to see if they recognized the man you shot at the hospital. We found something. He listed his employer as

Strategic Design Systems on a rental application eight months ago."

Josh grabbed the form from her hand. "What did he rent?"

"A backhoe from the hardware store. And he gave his address as 625 Cedar Ridge Road."

Lawson recognized that address. "Bree and Ashlee's grandparents owned a ranch on Cedar Ridge Road. The bank foreclosed on it years ago. But we've already checked that place out."

Cecile shook her head. "Actually, 625 is the abandoned property next door to the old Taylor place."

Josh shook his head. "That can't be a coincidence. Cecile, call and find out who owns it now."

"I already did. It was purchased from the city four years ago by Strategic Design Systems. In fact, Strategic Design Systems recently purchased six foreclosed properties from the city."

"What does a software design company need with old abandoned farms?"

"They don't—not for any legitimate business, anyway. If Bree's old boyfriend was really working with them, he would know when the property was foreclosed on and could have passed along that information."

Josh sighed and glanced at the mounting evidence of a major trafficking operation taking place right under their noses. "I can't believe this is happening in my county. We knew there was some drug trafficking going on. Mayor Baxter and I have been going back and forth with ways to combat it, but I never would have imagined things had gotten this far out of hand."

Colby slapped his shoulder. "A small town like this with lots of foreclosed and abandoned properties would be a trafficker's dream. A lot of these old ranches would have enough buildings for storage and manufacturing as well as plenty of land for planes to come and go with very little scrutiny—not to mention other kinds of vehicles. Nobody blinks an eye when a truck rolls through with a trailer of any kind. They could move drugs in and out of here all day long and who would know it?"

Josh let out a deep breath. "Colby, phone your contacts in the DOJ and DEA and tell them to get to town ASAP. We're going to need a lot of help on this."

"On it," Colby stated, pressing his phone to his ear and walking out.

He turned to Paul. "We need to get eyes on

that property to confirm that's where they're holed up. Can you take point on that?"

Paul nodded. "Will do."

Lawson leaned toward his brother. "I know you're looking at the big picture, taking this drug operation down, Josh, but rescuing Bree and Ashlee is still our first priority, right?"

"Of course. We'll get them out."

Lawson walked out of the conference room. He believed his brother had every intention of keeping his word, but with the inclusion of the DOJ and DEA in the investigation, he prayed Bree and Ashlee's safety wouldn't get overlooked.

NINE

Lawson drove to the old Tillman farm with Paul. They parked on a hill that overlooked the main house and the major outbuildings. Paul pulled his duffel from the back of his truck and unzipped it. Inside was his SEAL gear along with a variety of weapons.

Lawson knew his brother had been well trained by the SEAL teams to infiltrate and rescue hostages in even the most dangerous locations. Josh had been right to task him with organizing this siege. Paul was better trained for the task than anyone else and Lawson was grateful he was involved given that both Bree and Ashlee's lives were at stake.

Lawson grabbed a pair of long distance binoculars and got down on the ground beside his brother to scan the property. Cars were parked around a building behind the house that looked to be a large garage enclosure. He spotted a black SUV like the one from the grocery store security feed. "That's where they are," he said.

Paul took the binoculars and scanned the area.

"I agree. The garage has the most movement and also the most security." He pointed to two large trucks parked by the barn. "That must be where they hold their product. It's quite an operation."

"And one that's operated for who knows how long right under all our noses." Lawson scanned the area and saw men walking back and forth from the garage to the barn. He also spotted two-men teams standing outside each of the side doors of the garage. "I see two guards each on the side entrances. I don't see any weapons, but I'm sure they're there. And if there's a back entrance, I'm sure that's well guarded, too."

Paul nodded. "They've got this place locked down pretty well. We'll need a coordinated course of action for our breach." He pulled out his camera and started snapping pictures. "Let's get these back to the sheriff's office and work out a strategy."

He stood and Lawson balked. "We're leaving?" They were staring at the place where he was almost certain Bree and Ashlee were being held hostage. Leaving without them didn't make sense to him. "We need to go get them before they move them. Or worse."

"If we try to breach that compound on our own, all we'll manage to do is get ourselves—and probably them—killed. The moment we go down there, we'll be in a fight and we'll need more firepower than the two of us have." He took out his phone. "But if it'll make you feel better, I'll have Josh send a deputy here to watch the compound and alert us if the women get moved before we get back."

He still didn't like the idea of leaving, but his brother was right. They couldn't go in there guns blazing without backup. They needed a plan if they were going to get Bree and Ashlee out of there alive.

Deputy Simmons arrived within fifteen minutes, prepared to stand watch while Lawson and Paul returned to the sheriff's office.

When they walked inside, Josh, Colby and Cecile were already looking over the photos Paul had texted to them.

"We spotted eight men coming and going from building to building," Paul explained. "Plus however many are inside. That's quite a large organization."

"What's the ETA on DEA arrival?" Lawson asked.

Josh's face looked grim. "They're currently working another operation and can't get a team here for eight hours."

"We don't have eight hours," Lawson protested. "Bree and Ashlee will probably be dead by then." He hoped Josh wasn't suggesting they wait that long.

Paul stood up for him. "Lawson is right. We can't put this off. We'll have to go in with just our own team."

"It'll be dangerous," Josh stated. He rubbed his chin and sighed. "But I agree—we have no choice. At least with the sun setting, we'll have some cover. I'm going to call the neighboring sheriff's offices to see if we can't get some assistance from them."

Lawson, Paul, Colby and Cecile worked out a strategy while Josh phoned around to gather more deputies to help. Lawson was happy to see so many willing to volunteer, including Deaver, Marks and Mahoney. And he could always count on Cecile to be front and center when needed.

He phoned Deputy Simmons for a status update.

"No one has come or gone from the compound since you and Paul left. Everything seems quiet."

"Okay, hang tight. We're on our way to you," Lawson told him.

He gathered his supplies, weapons, ammunition and vest and loaded them into his truck. The darkening colors of the night sky reminded him of that night standing beneath the stars with Bree and how right that moment had felt. He wanted another chance to make it happen.

God, please keep her safe until I can get her home.

He was worried. The kidnappers had their money. How long would it be before they decided Ashlee and Bree had both outlived their usefulness? Or had they already done so? He tried not to think that way. He had to work based on the assumption that both women were still alive.

Instead of driving himself crazy worrying about the danger they were in, he focused on the mission ahead. He was only a small-town deputy. He didn't have the skills or resources to work out a rescue plan like this, but God had seen fit to bless him with family who did. For that, he was thankful, and it seemed proof that maybe God was on their side.

He dug into his pocket for the note Ashlee had written him the night she'd left six years earlier. He'd read it a hundred times since. She'd called him unambitious and he was— according to her definition. He didn't want drama or action in his life. In truth, he was ready for nothing more than for this mess to be over. He wasn't cut out for all this excitement and danger the way his brothers were. His only reason for still being involved was that someone he cared about had been taken from him and he was determined to get her back.

He crumpled up the note and tossed it onto the floorboard. He didn't need it any longer. Those words no longer stung him because he realized the truth. She'd been right to leave him. He and Ashlee had never been a good match.

His phone buzzed and he scooped it up. It was Simmons calling with an update. His voice was full of excitement and his words were rushed, causing Lawson's heart to pound against his chest. Something major was happening.

"Another car arrived at the compound and you'll never guess who just got out of it."

Bree sat silently, her sister lying against her shoulder, dreaming of the simpler times on the ranch with Lawson. Her memories were edging back to her, beginning with the sheer terror of discovering Ashlee had been kidnapped and then finding Travis dead from an overdose.

Everything was still kind of fuzzy, but she recalled meeting with the kidnappers at the old barn and offering to return the money to them, but first, she'd insisted on seeing her sister. They hadn't taken her proof-of-life demand well and had opened fire, leaving Bree no choice but to hop back into the car and drive away without Ashlee.

Then she'd just blocked it all out.

Shame filled her and tears pooled in her eyes. Everything Lawson said about her was turning out to be true. She'd been the one to get them into this mess and then she'd left her sister captive with killers and conveniently forgotten it. Well, that wasn't the type of person she wanted to be any longer. "I'm sorry I forgot about you," she told Ashlee.

Her sister sat up and looked at her. "It wasn't on purpose, was it?"

"Of course not, but the doctors said it wasn't physical trauma. It was something in my mind that I blocked out. How could I have possibly blocked you out when you were in so much danger—when you needed me to find help and come back for you?" She was struggling to understand that, struggling to find the reason behind it.

Ashlee pushed a strand of hair from Bree's forehead and wiped away a stray tear with her thumb. Her face held no animosity toward Bree. "It's not your fault."

"It *is* my fault. All of this is my fault. Travis. The kidnapping. How did they get you, anyway?"

"They grabbed me in the parking lot. I'd just gotten back from my date. You loaned me this dress, remember?"

Ashlee's outfit wasn't in the best shape anymore—not after several days of being held captive—but the longer Bree stared at the dress, the more the memory came into focus. "It wasn't a loan—I gave the dress to you," Bree answered. "Travis bought it for me—said it matched my eyes. I used to wear it all the time. There are probably two dozen pictures on Facebook of me in that dress. I didn't want it anymore after things ended between us, but it was too nice to throw out. You said…"

"I said it matched my eyes, too—so I'd wear it through some new memories until you were ready to take it back."

"That's why they took you," Bree realized, numb with horror. "You were wearing my dress. That's why they thought you were me."

Ashlee nodded reluctantly, clearly not

wanting to upset her sister, but not wanting to lie, either. "It was an ambush. They had me shoved into the back of a van before I even knew what was happening. When they started talking about Travis, I realized that they thought I was you—"

"And you let them think that, so you could protect me." Bree shook her head, disgusted with herself as a lump formed in her throat. "Once again, my bad choices come back to ruin things for you."

"Some things are out of our control."

"And some things aren't. I've made a mess of my life." She turned away from her sister as shame and regret burned through her. She'd made this mess, but her sister was suffering the consequences.

Ashlee's voice when she responded was soft and merciful. "No, that's all in your past, Bree."

"How can you say that when you've been abducted and beaten because of me?" She would never forgive herself for the mess she'd made and neither should Ashlee.

Her sister gave an exasperated sigh at Bree's refusal to excuse her actions. She forced Bree to face her, a hand on each of her arms as her eyes probed Bree's. After a moment, her expression softened. "You don't remember all of it yet, do you? Travis has been out of your life for a while now, Bree. You left him and that life behind you when you found Jesus. It's because of Him that you've made all these changes to your life."

Ashlee's words made no sense to her and she sniffed back tears that were threatening to break free. "Jesus doesn't want someone like me, Ashlee."

"He does. He loves you, Bree, and so do I."

Bree fell into her sister's arms and clung to her. She'd always known Ashlee's love was unconditional, but how could someone like Jesus want someone as broken and flawed as her? And it wasn't only Jesus that didn't want her. "Lawson doesn't want me, either."

Her sister didn't flinch at her subtle confession of her feelings for Lawson and gave no indication of jealousy that Bree had fallen in love with Ashlee's old flame. "I'm sure that's not true. He's a pretty smart guy. He ought to know a great catch when he sees one."

"You're the one he wants, the one he's always loved. When we get out of here—"

Ashlee shook her head, fear filling her face as she recalled the horrible truth of their situation. "These men don't have any intention of letting either of us go."

Bree knew that, but what her sister needed

now was reassurance. Ashlee had already been through so much. "Everything is going to be okay," Bree told her, stroking her hair for the added comfort.

But Ashlee wasn't going to be easily placated. She straightened and looked at Bree. "How? They want that notebook, and we have no way of giving it to them."

"I wouldn't say that. I actually have a good idea where Travis might have hidden it."

A commotion outside the door grabbed her attention.

"What's happening?" Ashlee cried, but Bree had no idea.

The sound of keys jangling indicated someone was coming. Bree stood and pulled Ashlee to her as the door opened and the man who'd met her at the grocery store—she'd heard someone call him Lenny—stood in the doorway, a gun trained on them both.

"Let's go," he demanded. "The boss is here and he's ready for you."

Ashlee shivered beside her and Bree could feel the fear rolling off her. "He's horrible," Ashlee said in a low voice so only Bree could hear her. "He ordered his men to beat me until I talked, only I didn't know anything."

Anger slid up Bree's spine at the idea of what these men had done to her sister. And it was all this man's fault. He was the one in charge, the leader of this drug ring, so he was the one who would have to answer for her sister's injuries.

She grabbed Ashlee's hand and marched out, anxious to put eyes on the man responsible for all of this. She'd met him before at her initial attempt to buy back her sister's freedom, but her memory of him was still blurry and unfocused. He'd been a shadow at the meeting, a figure that his goons turned to for confirmation and orders.

They were led from the storage closet and into the larger room.

"Bring them over here," a man instructed and Bree bristled at the familiarity of his voice.

Lenny pushed them both forward. As two of his goons moved out of the way, Bree finally got a good look at the man behind all of the attempts on her life and the abduction of her sister.

Mayor Don Baxter.

"Are you certain it was Baxter?" Josh asked Simmons after Lawson put him on speaker-phone.

"I'm sure," Simmons said. "He wasn't even hiding. He drove right up to the garage and got out. The men at the doors didn't even flinch as he walked inside."

The sheriff's office door swung open and Cecile rushed outside to join them in the parking lot where they'd gathered around the phone. "I just called his house and his wife said he was working late."

"He'd have enough power to push the sale of foreclosed land through to his own shell company without raising any red flags," Colby stated.

Josh stepped away from the group, his shoulders slumped. "He's been in my office nearly every week pushing me to do something about drug trafficking in the county. Why would he do that if he was the one doing the trafficking?"

"To keep you occupied?" Cecile suggested. "That way, you'd be too busy with paperwork to do anything about his operation."

"Or maybe he came by to gather information and provide false leads," Lawson said, thinking about the way he'd sent them scrambling with the information about the biker gang.

Josh nodded. "I'd better alert everyone else about this new development. We don't want there to be any confusion about which side he's on when we enter that compound."

The group dispersed and Lawson got back into his truck. He'd seen indignation and anger brewing on his brother's face and he didn't blame him. Baxter had played them all for a fool, but that ended today.

Baxter's time was running out fast. The full weight of the Courtland County Sheriff's Office was coming at him.

It was time to snatch Bree and Ashlee from his clutches and bring them home.

"Well, well, well," Baxter said as he faced down Bree. "When my men here told me you'd come alone, I couldn't believe it." He glanced into the duffel bag she'd brought and smiled. "Thanks for the money. It's nice to have the amount returned, although it wasn't really what we were after. Travis had a notebook with some incriminating evidence inside that he was planning to turn over to the DEA. Of course, we couldn't let that happen. None of our usual persuasion tactics worked so we had to take something he cared about, Bree, in order to motivate him to return it. We assumed it would be in the bag with the money he was also returning, but my contact at the sheriff's office already confirmed that it wasn't there. I hoped you knew something about our missing item."

Learning he had a contact at the sheriff's office surprised her, but she'd already known he was sneaky and deceptive. "That day at the sheriff's office, you pretended not to know me, but that was a lie."

"Yes, but I had no idea about the amnesia. That was a surprise to me. It was then I realized we needed to send you another message about having kidnapped your sister."

"And the tip about the biker gang?"

"Just a small lie to throw Josh and Cecile and Lawson off my scent. It worked, too. And speaking of them, how did you manage to get away from the Avery brothers?"

"I sneaked away. They didn't know I was coming."

"Very smart of you, Ashlee."

She bit back her anger at this cruel, two-faced man who'd deceived the Avery family. "I don't know anything about that notebook, but I do know where Travis liked to hide things."

He gave her an intrigued smile. "Go on, I'm listening."

"I can take you there. It's not far."

She'd expected him to jump on her offer, but he was cautious. "But you won't, will you?" he asked.

"I will. Once you let my sister go."

"I can't do that, Ashlee. She's my best chance at finding what Travis took from us."

"No, she's not. I am. You see, you've had the wrong sister this entire time. Your goons messed up. They kidnapped Ashlee, not Bree. That's why she couldn't tell you anything about Travis. She didn't know anything."

He looked surprised, but glanced behind her to her sister then back to Bree, and understanding dawned on his face. "But you do, *Bree*?"

She nodded. "That's right, Mayor Baxter. And I'm willing to take you there on the condition that you let Ashlee go."

Bree watched him, hoping for some sort of agreement on his part. He looked her up and down, sizing her up as he considered her offer. She stood firm and prayed he would take it. It was her only chance of getting Ashlee, who was sobbing behind her, out of this mess alive.

A phone rang. Lenny answered it, then approached Baxter. "Sir, it's the deputy. Says it's important. It can't wait."

Baxter turned away from Bree and took the call, holding it to his ear as he listened to the person on the other end. "I understand." He ended the call and handed the phone back to Lenny.

"I'd like very much to take you up on your

offer, Bree, but I'm afraid I can't." He pulled out his gun, then turned and fired at Ashlee. Bree screamed as Ashlee fell to the ground, clutching her leg as blood spilled between her fingers. Bree darted to her, but Lenny grabbed her and pulled her away.

"Why did you do that?" Bree cried, noting the pain in Ashlee's face along with paleness from the growing blood loss. Anguish flooded her and she aimed it all at Baxter. "I said I would help you—you didn't have to do that. She needs a doctor. I'm not going to show you a thing unless you take her to a doctor."

Baxter ignored her. "Lenny, put her in my car." He turned back to one of his goons. "If she tells me what I want to know, have one of your men drop her sister in front of the hospital. If she doesn't, let her bleed out, then dump her on the property somewhere and let the coyotes do what they do."

"No!" Bree cried. Her eyes hadn't moved from her sister.

Ashlee reached out a hand for Bree. "No, don't take her. Bree, don't tell them anything. They'll kill me regardless. Don't do it."

Lenny half dragged, half carried Bree out the side door as other men dragged Ashlee away. He shoved Bree into the backseat of an SUV. Baxter slid in beside her, his gun still raised and pointed at her as Lenny climbed into the driver's seat, started the SUV and took off.

"It's up to you," Baxter said. "Tell me what I want to know and maybe she can live. Don't and you're both dead."

Bree stared at him as they drove off. She didn't believe Baxter had any intention of getting her sister to the hospital. And, if her sister was dead, she might as well be dead, too.

The sound of gunfire inside the building forced them into action sooner than they'd planned. Lawson heard his brother's voice on the radio yell, "Breach! Breach! Breach!"

He moved toward the building, gun raised, along with Cecile and other deputies. They burst into the building as a group of men in the corner began shooting.

The gunfight was over in less than a minute as the overwhelmed drug runners dropped their weapons and pleaded surrender.

"We give up," one of the men shouted, encouraging the others to come out with their hands raised. "Don't shoot."

Josh motioned for several deputies to cuff the men as the others trained their weapons on the shooters.

"Go clear the rest of the building," Josh

commanded, and Lawson joined Colby as they searched the remaining rooms in the garage.

He pushed open every door, praying to find Bree behind each one. He shoved open the last in the hallway and held his breath. A woman lay in a heap on the floor. She was holding her leg and blood was pooling on the floor around her.

Bree.

He hurried to her, putting away his gun and turning her over before recognizing the dress she'd been wearing in the video.

Not Bree. Ashlee.

"How bad is it?" he rasped.

"He shot me, Lawson, and he took Bree."

"Who took her? Baxter?" He stood and called for an ambulance. She needed to be treated right away.

She nodded. "She told him she thought she knew where Travis might have hidden something."

"What is it, Ashlee? What do they want?"

"A notebook. He said Travis had incriminating evidence about their operation that he was going to turn over to the DEA." Pain crept into her eyes and she held her leg. "Where is she, Lawson?"

"I don't know, but I'm going to find her," he promised.

It was a promise he intended to keep.

Colby stopped in the doorway. "Is it…?"

"It's Ashlee. Any sign of Bree? She was last seen with Baxter."

Colby shook his head. "The rest of the building is clear. She's not here."

Colby knelt and tried to stop the bleeding in Ashlee's leg. Meanwhile, Lawson's mind was racing with worry. If Baxter had Bree, then once she told him what he wanted to know, he would have no more use for her.

"There's something else," Ashlee said between gasps of pain. "Baxter received a phone call just a minute before you arrived. He said the caller was a deputy. I think he told Baxter you all were coming. He knew to get out of the building fast."

Lawson locked eyes with his brother, then hurried from the room to find Josh. If what Ashlee was saying was true, there was a mole in the sheriff's office.

Bree sobbed into her hands as they drove, bumping along through abandoned fields. They weren't on a road.

Baxter shoved his gun into her side. "Now tell me what I want to know."

"Why did you have to shoot her?" she cried, determined not to tell this man anything. "You didn't have to do that. I was going to cooperate."

"I thought you needed some encouragement."

She stared at him and knew he had no intention of allowing her or Ashlee to survive. She should have known better than to think she could bargain with him. He'd only be able to keep up his persona as the good, trustworthy mayor if he killed both of them to keep his secret safe. She made herself a promise. He would get no information from her. The notebook Travis had stolen would remain hidden. Let him shoot her. She had nothing else to live for—she'd ruined her life through years of bad choices and she'd caused her sister's death.

He must have noticed that determination rising inside her because he changed tactics. "Tell me what I want to know or your sister won't make it to a hospital." When that didn't work, he changed strategies again. "Then maybe I'll drive to Silver Star next and kill your boyfriend."

Bree gasped and felt herself die inside. He'd already proved he wasn't afraid to kill. She still remembered how Ashlee had writhed in pain from the gunshot and how no one had moved to help her. Lawson could handle himself, but he wouldn't see Baxter coming. He didn't know the man was crooked.

"Good, good," he said, seeing that she was softening. "Now tell me where Travis liked to hide things."

"And you'll give me your word that you'll leave Lawson alone."

"You tell me what I want to know and Lawson will be fine."

"I can't promise it is there, but Travis always thought this particular hiding spot was brilliant. He kept everything important there."

"Where are we going, Bree?"

"An old cave at the east end of my grandparents' property. Travis, Ashlee and I used to play and hide in it as kids."

Baxter ordered Lenny to head in that direction.

Bree stared at the landscape through the SUV's windows. It was just what she remembered from when she was a kid. She'd spent a lot of time on this land. She knew it and had loved it once—she hadn't realized how much until it had been taken from them.

"How much farther?" Baxter demanded.

"Keep going until we reach a group of trees. Then we'll have to walk the rest of the way."

He nodded and Lenny kept driving until they reached the familiar cluster. She got out and headed for the trees, the others following behind. By now, she was certain Ashlee was dead. She had no illusions that Baxter would keep her alive, either, once she'd led them to the cave, but she would do whatever she had to to keep him from turning his attention toward Lawson. Lawson deserved a happy life with someone who loved him the way he deserved. She'd been fooling herself into believing it could ever be her.

She motioned behind some brush. "Here's the cave. Travis always used it to store things he didn't want to have stolen. He loved the idea of having a cave of his own."

Lenny pushed aside the brush and Baxter shone his flashlight into the small opening. "Wasn't he afraid of wild animals?"

"It's too small for most larger prey and the opening is covered."

Baxter motioned for Lenny to go inside first. The henchman grabbed the flashlight, got down on his hands and knees and crawled inside.

"You'd better hope it's there," he growled as Lenny pushed his large frame into the small opening.

But Bree was done being intimidated by him. "I can't do anything about it not being there. If it's not here, then I don't know where it is. There's nothing you can do to me to change that."

"This was in there," Lenny stated, backing out and handing Baxter a lockbox.

Baxter grabbed it, then shot at the lock until it gave. He took out a black notebook and tossed the box. He skimmed through the pages and smiled happily. He had what they'd come for.

Bree couldn't believe that was worth killing for. She couldn't resist asking, "So what's in the notebook that's so important?"

"This book has the names of all our clients and our safe houses. If Travis had given this to the feds, our operation would have been compromised. He said he wanted to turn his life around the way you did and maybe win you back."

Tears pressed her eyes. So Travis had been trying to get clean. That was some comfort to her.

"Did you kill him?"

"No. I would have gotten what I wanted from him before I killed him. It was like the police said. An accidental overdose."

"Fine. You got what you wanted. Now, let me leave. You don't even have to drive me back to town. I'll walk."

He slid the notebook into his jacket pocket. "Not so fast, Bree. We can't just let you leave. You know that, don't you? You've seen my face and you know about our operation. You're a witness. I can't let you go."

Her stomach sank, even though it was what she'd expected. She'd just hoped… Well, it had probably been stupid of her to hope in the first place. But she had to at least try to persuade him, for her sister's sake if not for her own.

"My sister. You promised you'd get her help."

"I'm sure she's fine. That call I took was from my guy in the sheriff's office alerting me that they were about to surround the place. I imagine they're there by now and Ashlee has been safely rescued."

Tears slipped down her face. She wasn't even sure if it was because her sister had been rescued or because Lawson and the others had come searching for them. Whichever it was, she wanted to believe what Baxter said was true—and really, why would he lie about that?

But then she realized just how coldhearted he could be. "You left your men back at the barn to be ambushed without even warning them, didn't you?"

He shrugged. "I'm part of a bigger organization. Most of those guys were brought in from outside of town. I can't afford to risk my own life for people I hardly know."

A shiver ran through her at his hard logic.

He wouldn't blink at killing her, either. "What are you going to do with me?"

"First, you're my insurance out of this county. I'm sure your sister was quick to tell the sheriff about me. I can't stay as mayor anymore—and I'll need a hostage to cover my exit. After that, who knows? I have some friends who dabble in trafficking more than drugs. I imagine someone as pretty as you would fetch a nice price on that market."

Bree shuddered at the thought. She would rather he just shoot her. She very nearly told him so, but knew it wouldn't make a difference. If killing her would save his own skin, he'd do it without hesitation. At this moment, he needed her alive to protect himself—and nothing she said would matter more to him than his own survival.

Lenny grabbed her arms and forced her back to the SUV, into the backseat. She wasn't surprised to be two-timed by Baxter. She'd never believed he was going to let her go. Never for one moment.

But she decided as the SUV roared to life that she was going to go down fighting. She didn't really want to die. She wanted to live, wanted the chance to finally do something good with her life. Even if she could never be with Lawson, even if she was certain he would take one look at her and shun her for the mess she'd made, she wasn't going to just let these men win without a fight. She knew how ruthless they could be. No telling what they might do to her if she didn't escape. She'd worked so hard to get her life back after all those years of watching it sour and worsen, bit by bit. She'd found faith, she'd found *herself*—and she wasn't willing to let that go. Her life was a gift that God had given her, and she wasn't going to let these men take it away.

Bree glanced out at the landscape as they passed it. Now was her chance to get free while she was unbound. They hadn't even forced her to put on her seat belt for the drive. She had all the landscape to escape into— and she knew these hills better than any of these men.

The only flaw in her plan was that she didn't know if they'd activated the child locks on the back doors. But then, she'd seen Baxter open the door from the inside. Maybe they hadn't thought of it or maybe they'd believed their guns would be enough to keep her under their control.

And maybe they would be. She might jump free only to have them shoot her. It was a risk she had to take. The future they had in mind for her frightened her more than dying. She wouldn't continue to be a victim any longer.

God, please be with me.

She grabbed the handle and opened the door. Just as Baxter realized what she was doing, she jumped.

Both men shouted at her to stop as the SUV screeched to a halt. She leaped to her feet and took off running as the sound of doors opening and closing reached her ears along with Baxter's shouts to Lenny to go get her.

Good, they weren't firing at her. They wanted to chase her down. That meant she might be able to hide from them long enough to escape. Maybe they would give up and let her go.

Or maybe they'll hunt you down and shoot you.

She couldn't think of that. She only had to figure out the perfect place to hide. She'd grown up here, on these hills, hidden from her parents and grandparents, and spent many hours alone soaking in the sunshine and learning the lay of the land.

Bree hurried up a mound and ducked into a bushel of trees, crouching down and stopping to look back as the two men spread out, guns raised to search for her.

She'd done it. She'd escaped them. Now, she only had to survive.

TEN

They captured and arrested six men and enough contraband to make even the DEA happy with their acquisition. It sickened Lawson to see a drug trafficking ring operating out of his hometown, on properties that good families had given their lifeblood to work, but he had bigger concerns right now.

Bree wasn't here, and there was a possible turncoat among them.

He let Colby pass that bit of information along to Josh, but as he glanced around, every deputy he saw was suspect. He didn't know who to trust. Someone in his own office had betrayed them by working with Baxter. He glanced at Cecile, who was demanding answers from one of the men they'd captured. She looked tough as nails and had always seemed completely loyal to Josh, but was it all an act? Had she been feeding Baxter information all along? His eyes moved to Deaver,

Marks and Mahoney. Any one of them could be the leak.

He marched over to where Deaver was loading men into the back of a van for transportation to the jail. Lawson grabbed one of the detainees by the arm and pulled him aside. "Where is she? Where is Bree Taylor?"

The man's only response was to demand a lawyer.

Frustration bit at him as he returned the guy to the van, then headed to the on-site ambulance where Ashlee, the real Ashlee, was being tended to. Thankfully, her injuries were not life-threatening. They'd gotten to her in time, but it looked like these men had put her through the wringer for the past few days.

She saw him and reached out from the gurney on which she was lying. "Lawson, did you find Bree? Is my sister safe?"

He glanced at the EMT, who gave him the okay to speak with her. "She's not here, Ashlee. Neither is Baxter. They must have gotten away as we breached the compound." They hadn't gone out the front entrance or else Lawson and the team would have seen them. "Any idea where he was taking her?"

"I don't. Travis took something from them besides money—a notebook. They thought I knew where it was. That's why…" She touched the bruises on her face. "Anyway, Bree thought she might know where he hid it, but she never told me where."

Lawson watched her talk and the odd thing was that he heard every difference in her voice compared to her sister's. He was used to the smooth, cool way Bree talked and it soothed him. Ashlee definitely had more of a lilt to her voice. How had he missed that?

She wrung her hands. "She sacrificed herself for me. I begged her not to do that, but she wouldn't listen. She was determined to put herself at risk."

He nodded, thinking of how she'd sneaked away from him to go help her sister. "She's good at that, isn't she?"

Ashlee took a deep breath before answering. "She is now." He could see she meant that in a good way.

Something had changed in Bree. She wasn't the same Bree Taylor he'd remembered and talked down about behind her back before he'd known she was Bree and not Ashlee. He kicked himself for his attitude, but he was glad to have confirmation that she had changed—that she truly was everything he now believed her to be.

"What happened back there? How did Bree

end up in your car with amnesia and all that money?"

Ashlee explained about the parking lot abduction—and the confusion over Bree's dress. "They thought I was Bree and when I heard who they were, I knew I had to play along and let them keep thinking that, not only for my sake, but for hers, too. I was hoping to keep her out of danger."

"You were looking out for her the same way she was looking out for you tonight."

"I guess so. Anyway, I know they called Travis. They told him that they had Bree and would kill me unless he returned what he'd taken."

"I thought she and Travis broke up. Had they gotten back together?" Lawson asked, telling himself he had no right to feel jealous.

But Ashlee was shaking her head. "No, they've been over for ages. She was just the only leverage they could use against him. They couldn't threaten to kill him—if he died without revealing his hiding place, then they might never get back what he'd taken. And there was no one else they could threaten other than Bree. She was the only person he'd ever cared about. That was why she stayed with him for so long. He did bad things, but he really did love her. She gets down on herself sometimes—thinks she isn't deserving of love."

Ashlee's stare felt oddly pointed and Lawson willed himself not to blush as she continued. "She doesn't get that she deserves someone madly in love with her—someone who'll appreciate how sweet and smart and loyal she can be." She paused, frowning. "I never thought Travis was right for her, but I did believe he'd do anything for her. I still don't understand why he never showed up at the compound."

"He died a few days before I found Bree," Lawson explained. "Accidental overdose."

She scoffed. "That explains it, then. He must have been in such a panic about Bree that he didn't pay attention to the dose. So Bree was stuck trying to negotiate my release by herself. She tried to make the trade, but she wouldn't give them the money until she saw me. It was all a ruse, though. The money wasn't all they wanted. I don't think they really cared about it as much as they did about the notebook Travis took from them."

"But you don't know what was in it?"

She shook her head. "No. They never told me that. Just kept insisting I knew where he'd hidden it. But Baxter did tell Bree it held incriminating evidence about their operation."

Lawson sighed and took off his hat, annoyance more than anything else eating at him. Annoyance at Travis for putting them all in this situation—for being involved with Bree in the first place. "So Travis started this whole mess and then died before he had to deal with any of the consequences. Bree should have left him sooner—or better yet, not gotten involved with him in the first place."

"Travis wasn't always bad. When we were young, he was a good kid. It wasn't until he got mixed up in drugs and dealing that everything changed. The drugs changed him. I think Bree always saw that young boy she fell for in him—but if he kept anything of himself from then, he only ever showed it to her."

"Wait, you knew Travis from when you lived here? He grew up here in Courtland County?"

"Sure. His father worked for my grandfather as head stableman. That was back before they lost everything. We used to spend all our free time together, running those hills on the back of the property. The three of us always had a blast back then hiding and trying to find each other."

"Why did I never know any of this?"

"This was before we started school. Momma and Grandma homeschooled us for the first eight grades, but then her health got worse and they sent us to high school in Courtland."

"Where we met."

"Yes. Bree was already half in love with Travis even back then. Once, I even found them kissing in this cave on the property. It isn't very big, but it was big enough…" She trailed off and looked at him. "The cave! That must be where Bree is taking Baxter. Travis was always fascinated by it when we were kids."

"Where is this cave?"

"On the east end of my grandparents' property by a cluster of trees."

Lawson started to turn away to find his brothers and share this new information, but Ashlee grabbed his arm.

"Do you want to talk about what's happening between you and my sister?"

He cringed. Even her words had a sharper tone to them. He should have recognized that. He should have seen the difference. "No."

She sighed and put her hand on her hip in a motion he recognized from when she'd been frustrated with him—another leftover from six years ago. He would know that gesture in a heartbeat, yet he hadn't seen Bree do it even once. That should have been a clue for him. He just hadn't been paying attention because he'd thought he'd finally gotten what he wanted—an Ashlee who fit perfectly into his life.

"I'm thankful you found Bree and helped her."

"I helped her because I thought she was you." Her eyes widened and he continued. "She couldn't remember who she was and we all just assumed she was you. And somewhere along the line, she made me care about her. She made me..." He took off his hat and pounded it against his leg in frustration. "She made me fall for her. But then we started to realize that she might be Bree, after all, and I pushed her away. I was angry, I was hurting—I lashed out."

Ashlee put her hand on his back. There was a time when just her touch would have sent him reeling with passion, but today her touch didn't make him respond.

"Let's face it, Lawson. What we had ended a long time ago. I am sorry for how it ended. I wish I had had the courage to leave earlier—and to tell you in person. I let it go on for too long because I did care about you. We were just too different."

Lawson nodded. He couldn't dispute her words. He'd come to the same realization.

He'd loved her, but at some point, he'd realized that it would never have worked between them. They'd wanted different things out of life. Yet he hadn't ever really been able to move on.

"I think I've been in love with the idea of you for a long time."

She nodded, seeming to understand what he was saying.

"I don't know what happened between you and Bree, but I trust in her, Lawson. I believe in her. God has changed her heart. She won't care that you lashed out. She'll forgive anyone she loves."

Ashlee had put her finger right on the thing he was struggling to admit to himself. He'd finally accepted that Bree was the one he wanted, not Ashlee. But would they be able to move past the harsh way he'd treated her? Ashlee seemed to think so. "And how would you feel about that?"

It shouldn't matter to him how she felt about it, but he wanted to know.

She smiled. "I love my sister and I want her to be happy. If you're the man who'll make her happy, then I think that's wonderful. But you don't need my blessing, do you?"

He shook his head. "No, we don't, but I sure would like it, Ashlee."

"Then you have it. Now, go find my sister and bring her home."

He slipped his hat on and flashed her a smile. "Yes, ma'am."

He hurried to find his brothers to work out a plan to rescue the woman he loved.

"Did she have any information?" Josh asked as Lawson joined them.

"She's not sure, but she thinks Bree might have taken Baxter to a cave on the east side of her grandparents' property. We need to spread out and go searching for Bree."

"We don't have the manpower for that, Lawson," Josh stated. "Not while we have an unidentified mole. Plus, we have to interview the men we captured. It's possible they'll have information about where their boss has gone."

"But until then, Bree is with him in danger. What if he has a plane stashed out there somewhere? If he takes off with her, we may never find her."

Paul spoke up. "Lawson's right. We need to start searching. Josh, you and Colby start interviewing these guys and see what information you can get from them. Lawson and I and two deputies will spread out and start searching. It's the least we can do."

Josh glanced around at the deputies. "Okay,

but take some of the Clayton County deputies instead of ours. We still don't know who we can trust and who we can't."

Lawson hopped into his truck and took off in the direction Ashlee had told him about, the abandoned Taylor Ranch. Paul and the Clayton deputies he recruited would try to cover the Tillman property. The manpower was spread thin and it would take time. Lawson was glad Josh had agreed to Paul's plan because he was determined to search regardless.

God, please keep her safe until I can reach her.

Bree ran, her mind focused on nothing but getting away from Baxter. Her side hitched, but she didn't stop. She tripped over a rock and tumbled down a slope, hitting the bottom. Pain rushed through her, but nothing indicated a specific injury—there was just a dull, aching, I've-had-enough-of-this-abuse reaction from her body.

She didn't move right away, choosing instead to stare up at the night sky, stars sparkling against a black backdrop. She couldn't recall the last time she'd seen a night sky so clear and bright. It was certainly a change from the overcast sky dulled by light pollution that she usually saw in Dallas. Out here, everything was so much clearer.

Even her life seemed more in focus in Courtland. If she survived this night, if Baxter didn't kill her, she knew in her heart and soul that this was the place she wanted to be. Going back to Dallas wasn't even an option. She never wanted to leave the clean air and countryside that she'd grown to love.

And Lawson. She didn't want to leave Lawson. But she wouldn't have a choice about that.

Her heart broke at what she was losing. She hadn't meant to fall for Lawson and she knew she could never be with him. He'd made his opinions about her clear many times. He didn't care for her or the way she'd lived her life.

Her regrets poured over her despite the verse in Romans that said there was no condemnation in Christ Jesus. She'd clung to that verse after leaving Travis and her old life behind for good, yet it seemed someone was always trying to remind her of her past mistakes. Only Ashlee had been on her side. Her sister had always been there for her even when she didn't deserve it. No, especially when she hadn't deserved it.

It gave her some comfort to believe Baxter when he said Lawson and the others had raided the compound and rescued her sister.

God, please take care of Ashlee and Lawson. I pray for a happy life for them and a bunch of happy children.

It was the life she'd hoped for, dreamed of for herself, but it was never to be. Lawson would never forgive her for not being the woman he truly loved—and for being the cause of all this turmoil.

God, please help him to forgive me. I never meant to hurt him.

I love him.

"There she is!"

The booming voice above her sent her scrambling to her feet and taking off running, but this time, Lenny was right behind her. He tackled her to the ground, pressing the gun against her until she stopped fighting.

She heard the squeal of brakes and the door of the SUV slam as Baxter approached. "Don't do that again," he demanded, taking her arm and dragging her to the SUV where he shoved her into the backseat. Once inside, he barked at Lenny, "Head to the plane. We're getting out of here now."

Lenny jammed the vehicle into gear and took off.

Bree knew her time was limited. If Baxter

got her on that plane, as soon as he got out of the state, he would kill her and possibly dump her body—or worse, turn her over to that trafficking guy he'd mentioned. She had to get out of this SUV and get out now.

She glanced at Baxter who seemed to sense what she was thinking. He raised the gun just as Bree kicked at him. The gun fired, but the bullet whizzed past her and through the driver's head before cracking into the windshield.

She kicked at Baxter again, knocking the gun from his hand. He scrambled to pick it up.

They'd sped up as Lenny slumped over the steering wheel, his foot still pressing down on the gas pedal. She had to stop the SUV from roaring out of control or get out of it before it was too late. She reached over the front seat, but the blood spatter on the window told her Lenny wasn't just wounded. He was dead.

Baxter swore and grabbed her shirt, pulling her back into the seat where he backhanded her, slamming her against the door. Her head hit the glass and a sharp pain ripped through her, causing her to gasp for air. Darkness danced around her eyes. She was losing consciousness, but she was alert enough to know the SUV was careening wildly.

Baxter leaned over the seat to try to stop

the vehicle, but the tires hit something and the SUV flipped, over and over again.

Bree couldn't even scream as it splashed down into a lake until water began to seep in.

Fear covered Baxter's face as he tried the door. It wouldn't open, so he tried to crawl into the front seat.

Bree knew she had to try to escape, but she couldn't move. She couldn't do anything but pray as water seeped into the vehicle and the darkness pulled her down.

Lawson had to find her before Baxter escaped. She wouldn't survive if he managed to get away. Baxter had the means to disappear. Plus, it was getting dark, which would make finding them even more difficult.

Lord, please help me find her. He had so much he wanted to tell Bree. He loved her. He'd known since the first time she'd touched his face that he wanted her in his life, but fear had kept him at bay, fear that she would reject him, fear of not being enough for her.

He knew now why he and Ashlee had never worked. They wanted different things. But Bree... Bree was just the woman for him and he couldn't wait to ask her to marry him and stay at the ranch with him.

But first he had to find her.

His headlights spread across the lake and he spotted something in the water. He pulled up and turned on his high beams. It was the tires of an overturned SUV.

He grabbed his phone and shot his brothers a quick text, then hopped from the truck and ran to the bank as he spotted something moving in the water. A moment later, Baxter, his clothes soaked and his head bleeding, waded out.

"Where is she?" he demanded. The mayor's only answer was to gesture back to the vehicle in the water.

"She fought me. She tried to get away. The gun went off and shot Lenny in the head. I couldn't get control before it flipped and landed in the water."

"And Bree? You just left her there?"

Baxter slipped out of his wet jacket and ignored the gun Lawson raised at his head. "She hit her head. Lost consciousness. She's probably still alive down there. You have a choice, Lawson. You can rescue her or stand here with that gun trained on me until she's dead."

He gripped the handle of the gun tighter, but he knew Baxter was right. He needed to reach Bree and get her out of that water before she drowned. But he wasn't ready to let this man go, either.

Baxter grinned and rubbed water from his hair. "What's it going to be, Lawson? Do you care more about taking me in or rescuing the girl?"

Baxter kept his eyes on him, then Lawson noticed something in his hand. As he started to lift his arm, Lawson realized what it was. A gun!

Baxter raised it toward him and Lawson fired, hitting Baxter in the leg. He dropped the gun, screamed out in pain and fell to the ground, grabbing his leg as blood began to redden his wet trousers.

Lawson walked over to him and picked up the gun, tossing it into the water.

"My brothers are on their way," he said. "You stay right there." He could handcuff Baxter to his truck, but the man would surely fight him and that could cost precious moments Bree might not have. Instead, he kicked off his boots, then waded into the water to rescue Bree. The gunshot wound might not stop the mayor from fleeing, but it would slow him down and give his brothers a better shot at tracking him if he managed to get away.

He swam out to the overturned SUV and

saw the driver. Baxter was right. It was too late for him. The bullet to the head had probably ended his life immediately, but it hadn't stopped him from bloodying up the water.

He glanced through the back window and saw Bree still in the backseat. She wasn't moving. He tried the door but it wouldn't open, so he swam around to the other side. He had to get to her. Fear pressed at him.

That door wouldn't budge, either, but he spotted another window that had been kicked out. If that was how Baxter had gotten out of the car, Lawson could use it to get in. He pushed through the window and reached inside for her. She wasn't moving, which wasn't a good sign. He had to get her out. He grabbed hold of her, pulled her through the window and into the open water until his feet touched dirt. He carried her to the bank. She wasn't breathing so he started CPR.

She's not dead. She's not dead.

His mind was racing with what he would do if he lost her. He'd never had the chance to tell her he loved her. He couldn't lose her now. Not now after he'd finally gotten her back.

He glanced around. Baxter was gone. One less thing he had to worry about.

Headlights filled the darkness and he saw Colby, Paul and Josh hop from a truck and run his way. Paul pushed him aside, taking over compressions as he watched.

Colby draped a blanket over him. "What happened?" he asked Lawson.

He shook his head, his mind a jumble of thoughts and fears. "The mayor. He pulled a gun on me, so I shot him in the leg. He won't get far."

Colby nodded to Josh, who got on his phone and started shouting orders to organize a search for Baxter. He wouldn't get away. Not with the Avery brothers after him. He was most certainly leaving a blood trail for anyone to follow. A good bloodhound should be able to flush him out with no problem.

But Lawson couldn't focus on that now. He would leave Baxter and his crew to his brothers. His sole focus now was the woman lying unmoving on the ground. What would he do if he lost her?

He hadn't even known his heart could sink so low, but every second Bree didn't respond to the CPR was a second his heart fell even further. Despair began to set in and only fear kept him from pushing his brother out of the way and swooping her up into his arms—fear that she wouldn't respond to him, fear that he would lose it when he touched her.

He put his head in his hands and just

prayed. It was all he could do for her. He'd never been able to save her. Only God could do that and if He chose not to save her life here, at least He would save her soul. But how was Lawson going to go on without her in his life?

She flinched and then started coughing and gurgling up water.

Relief flooded him. Relief and gratitude. This time, he *did* push past Paul and put his arms around her. He covered her with the blanket Colby had given him.

"Bree. You're okay. You're going to be okay," he told her, planting kisses on her forehead.

She lifted her hand to his face. "Lawson?"

"I'm here. I'm right here. I'm not leaving your side. I thought I'd lost you."

She leaned her head against his arm. "I shouldn't have left you. I had to—I had to save my sister."

"I know."

"Ashlee?"

"She's okay. She's at the hospital. She's safe." He pushed the hair from her face and nearly lost his composure. He was just so happy she was alive. "I love you, Bree," he whispered, but he wasn't even sure she heard his declaration before she faded away again.

* * *

Bree hugged her sister tightly. She didn't want to let her go. It had been wonderful being with her again the past three days, but today Ashlee was returning to Dallas and back to her own life. Jake had shown up to be with her and the money he'd given Bree had been returned to him. Ashlee had confided that she thought this relationship was going somewhere. She didn't blame Bree for what had happened and made Bree promise not to blame herself.

"Take care of her," Ashlee said, speaking over Bree's shoulder.

Bree turned around to see Lawson leaning against the porch post, legs crossed in his easygoing manner.

"I will," he said. He moved down the porch steps. "By the way, I had a voice mail from the manager of your apartment complex. They found your cat after he got loose and are taking care of him until you return."

"Thank you. I can't wait to get back to him."

He gave Jake a handshake and Ashlee a hug. "You be safe."

"Don't worry about me—I'll be fine." She fiddled with Bree's hair, then smiled. "But I'm thinking of adopting a new hairstyle just in case there's any more confusion in the future." She gave Bree a wink, then turned and allowed Jake to help her to the car. They drove off together.

With effort, Bree reminded herself she didn't have to worry about Ashlee's safety anymore. Mayor Baxter had been captured and arrested. The SUV had been pulled from the lake and the recovered notebook had listed the names and addresses of all the ring's suppliers and dealers across the country. According to Colby and his friends at the DOJ and DEA, the book and Baxter's arrest would bring down one of the biggest drug distribution operations in the country.

Bree was glad of that, glad that people like Travis would no longer be trapped in addiction because of people like Don Baxter.

But all was not well with the Courtland County Sheriff's Office. Baxter's phone records revealed he'd received a call from Deputy Deaver shortly before he'd fled. Kyle Deaver had left the scene of the compound only to be captured in a drug den in Dallas as part of a DEA sweep. Ironically, the raid had resulted from information obtained from Baxter's notebook.

"What do you think about him?" she asked

Lawson as Jake and Ashlee's car kicked up dust in the driveway.

He shrugged. "I'll admit I didn't want to like him at first, but he checks out okay. Plus, he seems to make your sister happy."

"Yes, he does."

"I'm hoping I can do the same for you." He slipped his arm around her and she flinched and pushed away.

"I'm not sure that can happen." She walked onto the porch and fell into a rocker.

Bree watched as Lawson took off his hat and fidgeted the brim with his fingers before following her and taking a seat on the porch step. His declaration of love for her on the banks replayed in her mind all the time and made tears press at her eyes with every word. Her heart hurt so badly, wanting to believe him, but she knew too much had happened between them to make a future together.

She choked back tears as she thought about leaving this place. She'd fallen as much in love with Silver Star Ranch as she had with Lawson Avery.

"What's going on with you, Bree?" he asked, not turning to look at her.

Her heart soared at the sound of her name on his lips, but then instantly fell at the thought of leaving here. She thought he would be happy to have a way out of his declaration of love, a way to save face. He turned to face her and she wiped away a tear that slipped through. "I love it here. It's beautiful. But I can't stay. You know I can't stay."

"Why not?"

"You know why. I've done too many things, messed up too many times. You said it yourself. I'm bad news."

"I was wrong, Bree. I judged you for things I knew nothing about. I'm not so perfect, either. I spent the past years chasing after something I thought I needed—a career outside of Silver Star and a woman who didn't even want me. I was so blind to what I already had, and what I truly needed.

"The truth is that everything I've ever wanted is right here on this land today and that includes you. You're not that person I was foolish enough to believe you were. You're a beautiful, smart, loyal and courageous woman who I want to spend my life with." He rubbed his hand through his hair and sighed. "When I thought I'd lost you, all I could think of was getting you back safe. I couldn't bear the thought of my last words to you being so vile and bitter."

"You weren't wrong."

"Yes, yes, I was. Don't you see, Bree?

You've changed. Everyone keeps saying it. Maybe it's time we both accept it. Neither of us is perfect, but we've both been made perfect by the blood of Jesus. He's washed away all our sins and made us new creations." He got up, then knelt beside her rocker. "New creations that belong together." He pulled something from his shirt pocket and opened it, holding it out to her.

Tears filled her eyes as she stared at the lovely diamond ring. "It belonged to my grandmother," he explained. "I know it's not much, but I want you to have it, Bree. I don't want you to leave. I want you to have all of this with me." He took it from the ring box and held it out to her. "Will you marry me, Bree Taylor?"

Her chin quivered at the sight and she bit her lip to keep from bursting out a yes. "Are you sure you're asking the right twin?"

"I've never been surer of anything else in my life. You're the right twin for me and the right woman in my life. Please say you'll marry me."

So many emotions pushed at her as she stared into his eyes. But her doubts finally fled when she saw acceptance and love settle there. She nearly couldn't catch her breath as she gave him the answer he was waiting for.

"I would love to be your wife, Lawson. Of course, I'll marry you."

Her hands shook as he slipped the ring onto her finger, but he settled them. They both stood and he pulled her into his arms and kissed her, sealing all her doubts away once and for all. She leaned into his arms and knew this was the place she always wanted to be.

"Promise me one thing," she told him. "Promise me we'll never leave this land."

He slipped his hat back on and pulled her closer for a kiss as he whispered, "That's one promise I intend to keep."

* * * * *

Dear Reader,

Thanks so much for joining me on this brand-new adventure. This is the beginning of a new series for me entitled Cowboy Lawmen and *Texas Twin Abduction* is book one. I hope you enjoyed reading it as much as I enjoyed writing it.

At the heart of Lawson and Bree's story is the theme of second chances. Lawson thought he wanted a second chance with his ex-fiancée, Ashlee, but he soon learned he was trying to force something that would never happen. Bree's past seemed to define her until she realized that our God is truly the God of second chances. Together, these two very imperfect people found their second chance at love.

I love hearing from my readers!

You can contact me online through my web site www.virginiavaughanonline.com or on Facebook at www.Facebook.com/gin-vaughanbooks.

Virginia

ReaderService.com has a new look!

We have refreshed our website and
we want to share our new look with you.
Head over to ReaderService.com
and check it out!

On ReaderService.com, you can:

- Try 2 free books from any series
- Access risk-free special offers
- View your account history & manage payments
- Browse the latest Bonus Bucks catalog

RS19